Thanks for your love & support

Love, Ken.

Whispers of Heaven

and Other Spiritual
Adventures
from the Ancient City

Rev. Ken Wilcox

D1569088

Dedication

I have so many to thank.

To my loving and tolerant partner Tom. To the two angels on four paws that I live with, Sadie and Madison. To my wonderful niece, Amy and my beloved prayer partners Bev & Rev. Elizabeth Claire. I am also very fortunate to be part of an amazing spiritual community. Sundays are fun and inspiring and we're doing great good in the community. This wonderful community has supported me in becoming the person I had always dreamed I would be. I need to thank my friends from the St. Augustine

Interfaith Community: Rev. Amy Lehr Camp, Rabbi Fred Raskind, Rev. David Williamson and Swamini Radhikananda. Also, my dear friends from Atlanta: Dr. Joyce Rennolds and Rev. Paul Graetz. And finally, I want to thank St. Augustine itself - Historical and beautiful, but better than that, a friendly and wonderful place to live.

Many thanks and much love, Ken

Foreword

I began thinking about this book as Hurricane Matthew was threatening my hometown of St. Augustine, Florida. My partner and I had never been through a hurricane so when Matthew showed up at our doorstep, we grabbed our two dogs and headed to higher ground.

A hurricane is quite an experience. It's like getting a bad report from your doctor and then waiting for the follow-up exam. The waiting is the worst. As the storm approaches some people become stressed while others seem to find more of their humanity. The day before the storm the little lady at the bagel shop purposely touched my hand while giving me back my change. Looking me in the eye she said, "Keep yourself safe, sweetie." She had me at "sweetie."

The storm invades your life in stages. First you hear its name. Then you start getting details about its direction and strength. For a brief while "staying or going" becomes the only topic of conversations.

Then there's the preparation, which can be a lot of work. Boarding up the windows, getting water, gas and batteries. Finally, there's the food supplies. I noticed in our house there seemed to be a generous amount of Little Debbie's and Oreos.

Like penguins jumping from an ice shelf, preparing for the storm is a herd activity. Eventually there's a quick exit for those escaping and then an eerie silence and stillness descends. It's like being the last one at a party and suddenly realizing everyone is gone.

Where we live is not on the beach but is close to water. Twenty-four hours out from the storm we got the mandatory evacuation. With more concern about the dogs' needs than my own, I threw a few T-shirts in a bag and grabbed the one book I knew would keep me entertained and calm. It was James Herriot's <u>All Creatures Great and Small</u>. It was like grabbing a trusted friend on my way to the doctor's office.

As the storm raged over head and my friends gathered around the TV for the latest updates, I cracked open the pages of my book and found myself enveloped in the lush meadows of the Yorkshire Dales. Herriot's stories transported me from a place of turmoil to a land of kindly animals, and warm kitchens with sweet scones and fresh cream.

After the storm, I marveled at the idea how one lovingly written book had provided me a respite from my worries. Now almost two years later, I'm finishing writing my book just after our city has survived another brush with a hurricane. It seems to me that life has become a series of storms for many of us each crashing in on our consciousness barely giving us the time to recover before new clouds appear. Social media and the news have become cheerleaders to every fear and doubt, and we seem unwilling or unable to stem their toxicity.

I wrote this book in the prayer that it would be a cup of comfort for anyone experiencing turmoil.

If it provides you with a bit of encouragement and a chuckle for a moment, then God love it.

I have included affirmative prayers in the book. Please, don't allow them to scare you. Praying is the most natural activity in the world. It should come as easily to us as breathing. If it doesn't it's probably because someone frightened you with it as a child. It's time to get over that and step into your spiritual maturity. You're needed now on the front line of creation.

If something in one of my prayers works for you, hold tightly to it. If I write something that doesn't work for you, then just let it slide by.

If one of the prayers or even a statement from one appeals to you, try to memorize some part of it. It may be a few words, "Life is Good." Say it to yourself as often as you can, particularly when you are in a good place. When you're out with friends and laughing so hard that you have to catch your breath, say, "Life is Good." Do it when you get a great parking space or have a loving conversation.

If we will speak to God in our joy, we will build the faith to turn to Spirit in times of trouble.

If you do get a moment of joy from one of my stories, use that good feeling to send a healing thought about yourself to the heart of God. When you get bored of doing that for yourself, start doing prayers for your family, friends and even strangers. Say prayers for those you love, those you like, and even those you don't care so much for, particularly those you don't care so much for. Then do it for the world and when you see any improvement, even the smallest, shout, "Glory."

Now don't shout out in the middle of the grocery store, it scares people. I should know; they have my picture posted in the local cheese department. And you don't have to run all over the world telling everyone what you're doing. Keep it to yourself. There is power in your having a conspiracy with God to bring about a new heaven.

I understand many of us are completely fried by all the stress and confusion in our lives. But I also know that Spirit would not have created us for such times if we had not been given the strength to overcome any challenge. You plus God equals a majority in every situation you'll ever confront.

We have the gift to bring in a golden new era of kindness and community. We won't do it through guilt and shame. We've tried that for over two thousand years now. That falsehood came from our misunderstanding the ministry of Jesus. We can bring about a new earth and we'll do it with our joy, our love, and our compassion—just as Jesus taught.

It's in every one of us to do. Spirit has called you by name from star dust to be here at this moment. You and I are on a mission from God to make the best life possible. Our lives are not problems to be solved, they are miracles unfolding.

Dear Friend, believe in yourself, believe in the loving power of God, believe in your desires; they have the energy of the universe behind them.

And as the Divine Ms. M (Bette Midler) sang in a song years ago, "Keep your humor please, because don't you know in times like these, laughing matters most of all."

Introduction

I grew up with seriously mental people. My mom would quite accurately say about her brew, including herself, "They're throwing our soup out at Milledgeville every day" (Milledgeville being the state mental hospital). None of us ever had the energy or conviction to argue with her. Much of my childhood was spent anxiously awaiting impending doom, the Russians dropping the A-Bomb or Jesus coming back. I spent hours, perhaps even days or weeks, hiding under the rusted trampoline in the weed free section of our back yard. It seemed the safest place to be.

You couldn't have found a psychiatrist in town who would have not labeled us all buck-ass crazy. That's a formal diagnosis. You can look it up. Fortunately, we had the tendency to enjoy our insanity. We had fun with it. In my mind it's the humor that can save you. If you take life too seriously, you'll find yourself running buck naked down the middle of the street. One of us would actually succumb to such a temptation. It was reported live on the 11 o'clock evening news on all three local TV stations, but that's a story for later.

Macon, our hometown, would have never condoned such emotional excess in the middle of the sixties. In fact, it was such a repressed hotbed of tension, both sexual and racial, that the ladies, mostly white, insisted that the big department stores downtown only allow their black workers to handle the white mannequins by cover of night. The sight of a black man touching the plastic preformed body of a white woman just couldn't be countenanced in a Christian community.

Macon surprisingly had produced some real talent: Otis Redding, The Allman Brothers and Little Richard, to name a few. The mayor of the city also gained national fame by issuing a shoot to kill order against any civil rights protestor during the height of the civil rights movement. Nicknamed Machine Gun Ronnie, he was the first Republican mayor since Reconstruction. During his second term, President Richard Nixon came to celebrate the local law school and on stage pointed to Machine Gun and said, "I would like to see this man governor of Georgia one day." What Nixon didn't realize was that sitting directly behind him was a future president of the nation—Jimmy Carter.

Ronnie failed to gain the governor's chair. In fact, his political career was soon to implode when he developed a taste for amphetamines and came down with a nasty case of paranoia. There were rumors of the police having to be called out to his house to stop him from chasing his wife around the yard with a loaded pistol. Most voters were willing to give him a pass on such family indiscretions much like they would someone bringing a bowl of bad potato salad to a potluck. It's regrettable, but sometimes unavoidable.

The electorate finally got their fill of Ronnie when the area began to experience a rash of UFO sightings. My oldest sister swore one had tried to kidnap her. We were all so hopeful. Things got so out of hand during the summer of 1975 that Machine Gun gave a shoot to kill order against any UFOs disturbing the peace of Macon.

The city may have moved on past Ronnie, but he remained a hero in our family. To have that level of nuttiness and still be able to get a whole community of people to support you—well, it was just something that gave hope to each and every one of us.

In some families, the children distinguish themselves with varying levels of talents and proficiencies.

"Oh, Johnny is learning the classical flute, while Dorothy is state champion in team debating," some fawning mother might say. In our family we achieved notoriety with our varying levels of craziness.

My middle sister insisted that Macon had a crew of master shoplifters. To become a member of the crew you had to pass a critical test. You had to walk into the local K-mart and be able to walk out with a portable typewriter tucked between your knees.

I assumed the crew was mostly made up of Amish looking women, so for much of the fourth grade I would wander around K-mart following women in long skirts listening for the tell-tale sound of the clacking keys or the ringing of the return bell.

The sister just older than me was what we affectionately called our family's "wild child." She had a burning desire to either become one of the mermaids at the Weeki Wachee Springs resort in Florida or marry one of the Beatles. We all encouraged her to practice holding her breath. Of all of us she was the most likely to allow my mom to practice her brand of home healing. My mother had total confidence in her ability to heal any of us. It often required something painful, so most of us hid any injuries or weaknesses. Susie on the other hand was a willing guinea pig. Once with a bad flu she developed severely chapped lips. My mom thought it would be soothing to melt a tube of Chapstick and poor the molten wax on her protruding lips. The wax immediately froze her lips to resemble Donald Duck. As she ran around the house squawking, the rest of us (of course) fell on the floor laughing.

My mom was something of a comic genius particularly when she was hurt. Once before a family outing, she was the last to get ready. With her bra-girdle combination on, she sprayed under her freshly shaved arm pits what she thought was a can of deodorant. It happened to be a sample sized can of a new product that most of us would later come to know as Scrubbing Bubbles. She burst out of the bathroom flapping arms and legs. We all swore that she had on that day in fact invented the dance which was later to be called the "Funky Chicken."

My father wasn't very much of an entity in my family. He had a major heart attack when I was three. The doctors of the time encouraged him to avoid strenuous activity. He took to it like a duck to water. The "don't get him upset or you'll kill him," threat was a sword that hung over all our heads and was considered by my mother to be her masterstroke to the art of child domination.

Dad was to die in a car accident when I was thirteen. To a person, all of my siblings have admitted that on hearing the news we were all grateful that we had avoided personal responsibility.

Before his passing, he tormented us, and me particularly, with religion.

Sunday mornings, far too early, we were awoken with the very loud vocals of Vesta Goodman of the Happy Goodman Family. I can't tell you the times I have prayed that she would die of lockjaw.

After a breakfast of bland scrambled eggs, we were hauled off to the Napier Avenue Church of God. There they spoke in tongues, ran up and down the aisles and did everything but handle snakes, and for that the snakes were grateful. Weekly, they preached about the return of Jesus and the fate of sinners in everlasting hell fire. The problem was that none in our family ever professed to having the born-again experience, the only thing which could save you. My mom would have never tolerated such hypocrisy of goodness on our part.

Each week we went to hear how worthless we were and how soon we would be subjected to everlasting punishment.

The saving benefit to their services was that they sang well. My father said their singing made him feel like his hair was standing on end. He claimed to have had a similar experience during the war, when on a transport boat being unloaded on Okinawa, rockets were fired over his head at the Japanese embankments. It was the similarity of the experience that made him feel that he had discovered a place of God.

Just to ensure that I became a total neurotic my father decided that they should send me off to Macon Christian Academy. The hope was that I would become what is known in the South as a slicked-back-hair, fire and brimstone preacher. I think it was kind of his bargain Dad had made with God for having allowed him to survive his heart attack. Little did he know that he was well on his way to raising a raging heathen. My new school was run by dipped in the blood of Jesus sorts of people who didn't want their little white children going to school with black ones. I loathed them all. A particular target of my venom was the headmaster. Each Friday he hauled us into the auditorium of the school for assembly. There he would warn us against the evils of boys and girls swimming with each other, the dangers of the movies, and the eternal damnation for people using such words as heck, darn and shoot.

My mother cursed like a sailor, so I was sure that we were all headed to hell. It was during this period that I began to spend enormous amounts of my time under the trampoline waiting for Armageddon. Sometimes, I would jump on the trampoline, not for fun, but in prayer. "Take me, Jesus." I would pray. Hoping that a big celestial hand would come down and scoop me right out of all my misery.

No such salvation ever happened and at some point, climbing off the trampoline, I gave up on Jesus…a decision that would begin a twenty-five-year odyssey in what I would call my loudmouth atheist period. It made me very popular in Macon.

Now, here's the thing. Many years later through pain, sorrow, loneliness and addictions I would indeed come back to a spirituality, not the one that my father found, but a God of my understanding that would allow me to have a loving and encouraging relationship with Spirit.

In fact, I was to become the minister that my father had sought. Not the minister he envisioned, but one of a community where there is no damnation, no judgement, but love and compassion. A place where people leave feeling better and more hopeful.

What a journey it has been! From Macon, to Atlanta, to DC, to San Francisco, back to Atlanta, and now to St. Augustine, Florida, a spiritual journey from west of weird to east of orthodox. Now in this ancient city, I find myself perhaps living my father's dreams and even fulfilling my own, leading a happy band of pilgrims on the move in a joyful jubilee.

We all are on a wonderful
journey to know the very best for
ourselves. How do we join this
joyful jubilee? By proclaiming
the best of our souls. We are
Spirit's great gift to life.
Know this for yourself by saying
this prayer.

Affirmative Prayer

*I know that I am a Divine
being on the pathway of an
endless self-expression. The
eternal Good is my host, now
and forevermore. God has
called me by name from star
dust so that I could tread the
soil of the earth. I am on a
mission from Spirit to know
myself as that which is all*

loving, all good and all wise.
Spirit won't have it any other
way and neither will I.
I proclaim this right knowing
for myself
and release it into the Mind of
God.

Quaint Fishing Hamlet with a Slight Drinking Problem

The ancient city of St. Augustine, Florida is a charming seaside village the Spanish founded over 450 years ago. It has often been described as a quaint fishing hamlet with a slight drinking problem. I would be a reluctant witness as to how much fishing actually goes on here.

Our cobblestone streets are filled with musicians, artists, tourists and the occasional pirate or ghost thrown in for variety. The pirates and ghosts are generally, but not always, college kids from the local drama departments earning a few bucks.

During the Holidays the city puts up lights on the downtown buildings making it into a twinkling Fairy Land. The local New Thought Church which I lead—more about that later—rents a tourist train each year. We fill it up with people wearing elf ears singing Christmas Carols—sometimes even on key. We pile off at the main square to fill the gazebo. Our musical director brings his accordion and we soon have a chorus of tourists singing along with us under the lights strung from the massive oak trees. It could be right out of a Frank Capra movie.

On Christmas day we hand out gifts at a local assisted living facility. We get their names and wish lists from the administration. A couple of years ago, we noticed that a lady named Erma wanted a pair of size 43 corduroy pants and a bottle of Old Spice shaving lotion. A gentleman named Bud wanted a box of Estee Lauder facial powder and hand cream. We wondered what was going on and noticed that they shared the same last name. We realized they were getting each other presents so they would have something to exchange on Christmas Day.

As I've mentioned, I'm the minister at the New Thought Church here in town. If Oprah had a Church it would be us. We are a group of happy feel-good sort of people that make everyone suspicious. Actually, since they've recently passed the medical marijuana laws here in Florida, they seem to be a lot less curious. Although, I have noticed that at the Interfaith events we are always the ones asked to bring the brownies.

The truth of it is, that while we do have our share of odd balls and kooks, our Church and our city are a delightful place to visit and live. The nice thing is that we all try to tolerate and support one another.

When I first arrived some seven years ago, I began to be asked to give the opening prayers at the City and County Commissioners meetings. Yes, we still do that here in Northern Florida. Our city is run mostly by women. They are a smart, fashionable lot—fashion forward as they would say on Project Runway. The county is controlled by severely uptight white guys.

Now, the kind of prayers I do are always affirmative. I pray believing in our good, knowing that God is always supporting the best for us. I also pray for something immediate, something that will make this day go better. I make it practical and doable and I give it some energy and spirit. One of my friends says I am the Ethel Merman of affirmative prayers. If you don't know who Ethel is, look her up on YouTube.

The last time I was at the commissioners meeting, I prayed that we all would agree to act like adults. That in itself would be miraculous given the state of politics these days. I also prayed that we will be respectful of one another's opinions, those we agree with and particularly those we disagree with. I quickly wrapped it up—because nobody actually wants to hear a long-winded minister at these events—by saying that we would be mindful of one another's time.

Most of the time, my prayers are met by a stunned silence. I don't think they know quite what to do with me. Sometimes I catch the commissioners nervously eyeing one another contemplating who will be the first to dash for the exit. Strangely, they keep inviting me back. Their head administrator always thanks me for coming. He says the villagers, who can turn into a mob storming Frankenstein's castle if the right issue comes along, are always calmer when I'm there.

You have the great good sense to know what you need in life to make it go better. Share that great idea with Spirit. Believe in it with joy, love and expectancy. Our good is never hidden from us. There is always a practical and immediate way to allow the creativity of the Universe to flow in our lives. Say this prayer and then look for what's right in front of you to do to make the world a better place.

Affirmative Prayer

Today I uncover the perfection within me. I look out upon my affairs knowing that the Spirit within me makes my way both joyful and easy. There is no problem or condition which

cannot be resolved with the
wisdom of Spirit and my right
action. I listen to the still small
voice urging me on to my
highest good. I do what is right
in front of me to do and look
for a path before my feet to
reveal itself. My good is not
hidden from me,
but is seeking me as I seek it.

Bloodthirsty Alligator

I moved from Atlanta, Georgia to St. Augustine several years ago. I had only been living here for a couple of months when, on my way home from the office, I swung by the grocery store to pick up a quick dinner. This usually involves frozen fish sticks and tater tots. I know, living in a fishing city you would think I would have more refined taste, but there you have it.

As I was walking to the entrance of the store, I noticed a man passed out leaning against the wall. There was a plate of food in his lap, but what caught my attention was the condition of his right thumb. It looked like it was in a terrible state. From my distance I surmised it had been mangled by some bloodthirsty alligator.

Within just a few moments I had concocted an entire story about this poor man. I envisioned him passed out at one of our local ponds. While in deepest slumber he was awakened by a vicious reptile trying to make his thumb into a snack.

With mounting horror, I found myself unable to tear myself away from the gnarled flesh and exposed bone. When I finally got close enough to get a good look, I realized that it wasn't his thumb at all, but a chicken wing my happily slumbering friend had clutched between his thumb and hand. There was a grocery clerk standing nearby and he must have seen my distress, because he burst out laughing.

"That's from Betty in the deli," he explained. "She takes the food that's due to be thrown out and gives it to the guys who live in the woods behind the store. They'll fire her if they find out but she says she's not going to throw food out when there are hungry people about."

We both had a good laugh but here's the thing. In my thinking of all the dangers of St. Augustine I had conjured up a truly nightmarish situation of what had in reality been an act of compassion. When we allow our fears to get out of control, we can make a hell out of what really is a quaint little fishing village with a debatable drinking problem.

Use this prayer when you want to see and know better for yourself and those around you.

Affirmative Prayer

I know there is a Presence and perfect Law irresistibly drawing into my experience everything that makes life happy and worthwhile. This Presence I listen to and with this Law I work. I keep my thoughts elevated to my highest good. I see good in those around me. I give gratitude for their blessings. I encourage myself and others to listen to their souls' inspirations. The way is made plain before me

*and my journey is vouched safe
and secure.*

The Bra-Girdle Combination

The Church I lead is part of the Centers for Spiritual Living. We used to call ourselves the Science of Mind, but we got tired of people asking us if we were Scientologists. We're not, which is kind of unfortunate, because I've always fancied meeting Tom Cruise. The nice thing about our teaching is that we don't believe in one size fits all in spiritual growth. What works for you might not be the right fit for me. It's my joy to find out what calls to my soul.

Some people swear meditation is the answer to all spiritual quests. Dr. Ernest Holmes, our founder, emphasized praying affirmatively for oneself. I have found that the most powerful spiritual tool I have been given is a prayer partner. Someone who affirmatively prays for me and someone I can affirmatively pray for. There used to be a bumper sticker that said, "Let me be the person my dog believes me to be." My best Spiritual practice has been trying to be the person my prayer partner prays for me to be.

As you explore your journey you have to be careful not to try to squeeze yourself into someone else's spiritual path. You can't be like my mother. She had a favorite aunt, Vicky, named after the queen. My mom said that even during the worst of the Depression she would dress well, wearing large hats topped with artificial flowers and stuffed birds.

I can't say I really remembered how she dressed, but I do recall how nice she was. If you went to visit her as a kid, she made certain that you had something to eat even if it was nothing but graham crackers and milk. At some point in the early seventies while the country was still in Vietnam and Nixon in the White House, Aunt Vicky talked my mother into trying a regimen that she had used most of her life.

This technique, she insisted, would help a person keep better posture and would aid in breathing and digestion. Your clothes would fit better, you would keep your head lifted up, you'd have more energy and your husband would find you more interesting. Your kids would improve in school.

This elixir of self-improvement was the bra-girdle combination, brought to us by the friendly and innovative people of the DuPont corporation, the same people who created indoor/outdoor carpeting.

My mother was sold. On her next trip through the lingerie department of Sears and Roebucks she purchased the Playtex bra-girdle combination for the full-figured gal. On the box was a photo of a hopeful looking model lounging in said bra-girdle sipping a cup of tea. The product promised to be both comfortable for 18 hours and to lift and separate. Mom chose to try out her new regimen on the very following Saturday when we were all scheduled to go to a summer funeral in South Georgia.

In my childhood, there was nothing more dreaded than a family funeral in our homestead of Fitzgerald, Georgia. First, we would have to get up early to make the drive. Then we would have to stay at a house with a dead body stretched out in the living room for a couple of hours. TV and games weren't allowed. You were expected to sit in misery and silence to prove how much you loved the dearly departed. Then it was off to the church for a painfully long sermon accentuated by mournful singing. Finally, you'd go back to the house, fortunately without the dead body this time, to stand around for a couple more hours. With the day completely shot, we'd pile back into the car to begin the long drive home.

Much of the day would require that you'd have to be outside in dress clothes sweating while being attacked by mosquitoes and gnats big enough to tote away babies. South Georgia gnats will fly in every orifice of your body, right into your eyes or ears. My sister would swear that they would fly directly from a dog's behind to your mouth. I don't know how she knew, but it sounded right.

On the way home from this particular adventure, as we were drifting off to sleep with the car windows all down and the radio tuned to country music, the full force of the summer's night air blasting us from every direction, without any explanation my mom began to tug at herself, first her shoulders then her sides.

"She is having a fit," my oldest sister yelled out from her slumber. Mental health was always considered questionable in our family unit. "Didn't she eat aunt Edna's potato salad?" my middle sister shouted. "I saw it bubbling before they put it on the table."

Mom answered to none of it as she continued to struggle with some unseen phantom. My dad's driving was totally distracted as he swerved from side to side.

Finally, with one last heave she reached up with both hands between her legs and snatched off the girdle/bra combination. Holding it triumphantly in her hand she shoved it out the window. "The son of a bitch went for my throat," she yelled defiantly as she released it to the humid summer's night air and the South Georgia asphalt.

You are totally unique. One size fits all won't work for your Spiritual journey. Know the best for yourself, by proclaiming your good.
Say for yourself:

Affirmative Prayer

God knows me only as a Perfect Idea and that Perfection I now manifest. God's Law is written in my heart and I delight to do God's will. Today, I will laugh and encourage others to do so. I will look for joy, health and prosperity. If I can't see it for myself, I will encourage and look for it in others. There is no power on earth that can keep a God inspired idea from coming to life. So here and now, I proclaim my health as God inspired. I proclaim my joy, love and prosperity as God inspired. I see them as a reality and I live from them in faith.

Heavenly Hash

My mother was no June Cleaver. She was more Rosanne Barr, a little Peg Bundy, with a huge ladle of Paula Deen thrown in. She smoked generic cigarettes one after another—lighting a fresh one from the butt of the other. She believed her opinion was truth and it always needed to be heard no matter how badly it hurt. She only grudgingly tolerated anyone in her kitchen unless you happened to be unloading her dishwasher.

There was much I needed my mother to be that she wasn't but the one way she did love, and indeed she was excessive about, was with her cooking. She made it her business to know each family member's favorite dish. For my sister it was a pan of dressing (stuffing would have never dared shown its face on my mother's table). For me it was her fried chicken, and for my niece it was Heavenly Hash.

If you've never been so fortunate to have a piece of Heavenly Hash, it's comprised of excessive amounts of butter, pecans and a complete box of powdered sugar. Like any true Southern dessert, it is devoid of anything healthy or fresh.

I always assumed that the Hash was a very difficult concoction to make involving Dutch ovens and specialized spatulas. Last year when my niece was visiting from Japan, I thought it would be fun to get Mom's recipes out to make it. Amazingly, Heavenly Hash proved to be extremely simple.

Mom loved us extravagantly in the way she could. It wasn't always enough for the people around her but showing love the best way we can is really all that can be expected of any of us.

If you haven't noticed, we seem to be going through an exceptionally disruptive period of late. So, if you're feeling the need to show a little love to a family member, friend or even to yourself, let me recommend Heavenly Hash. It's easier than it looks, as sweet as it sounds, and right now we could all use a little more Heaven on earth.

Mom's Heavenly Hash recipe

Heavenly Hash Cake:
    2 sticks butter
    4 eggs
    1 c. chopped pecans

dash of salt

4 tsp. cocoa

2 tsp. vanilla

2 tsp. baking powder

2 c. flour

2 c. sugar

1 pkg. large marshmallows

Heavenly Hash Cake Icing:

1 pkg. 16oz. confectioners' sugar

4 tsp. cocoa

10 or more tbsp. heavy whipping cream

dash of salt

1 tsp. vanilla

4 tsp. melted butter

Mix together all cake ingredients except the marshmallows. Grease a foil-lined 8" x 13" pan.
Spread mixture into pan. Bake at 350ºF for 30 minutes. While cake is

baking, mix icing ingredients with mixer until thick. After cake is baked, top with large marshmallows. Put under broiler until marshmallows are melted. Pour icing over melted marshmallows. Let cool one hour before serving.

The easiest thing we can do to
help the world is to be loving.
Our loving hearts can be a balm
to any situation. When we allow
God's love to flow through us, we
can become a resource center for
the universe.

Affirmative Prayer

*I express love in such a
manner that it will embrace
and warm the heart of
humanity. It brings confidence,
faith and hope to everyone it
touches. This warmth goes
from me and heals every
situation I encounter, not with
words or action but with the
energy of loving thoughts. I see
life working out for myself and*

those around me. I choose to know the best for myself and my world. This consciousness of love generates an energy and vibration. It radiates from me and impacts my environment. I am grateful for this power and I choose to use it for Good.

Crappy Plate of Linguini

One of the cornerstones of our Science of Mind teaching is to be open to new ideas and adventures. One of our best-known ministers, Raymond Charles Barker, wrote, "New ideas are as essential for the mind as food and water are for the physical body".

Unfortunately, many of us decide early on what we like and what we don't. When presented with the possibilities of the new, we dig in our heals. I can remember when I was in the second grade, we switched from the paper that had wide lines to one with smaller ones. I completely rebelled and was determined to be as sloppy in my writing as possible until the teacher bent under my will and switched back. Mrs. Powell, who didn't especially care for my paper judgements, ignored my complaints and to this day it takes a course in hieroglyphs to read my writing.

People who are youthful and vital are always reaching for new experiences. Many years ago, we took my partner's Aunt Carmen on a tour of Italy. At the time, Carmen was well into her eighties. She had spent some of her early childhood in Italy and could speak some Italian. Of course, everywhere we went the Italians treated her like a long-lost sister. One chef in Capri had a strolling street musician come in and serenade her. She was a bit of a ham, so she relished all the extra attention.

On our last day in Rome, we returned to a restaurant where she had particularly enjoyed a plate of seafood pasta. When it came time to take our order she asked for linguine with sausage. After the meal it was apparent that she hadn't enjoyed the linguine as much as she had the seafood. When I chided her on her selection she said, "Sure, I could have ordered the pasta, but I wouldn't have enjoyed it as much as I did the first time. So now I have two stories to tell my friends: the great seafood pasta and the crappy plate of linguini."

Does it seem like life has been giving you a lot of crappy linguini of late? Use this prayer so you can see beyond appearances and reveal the great blessings life has in store for you.

Affirmative Prayer

Today I speak Good into every experience I have. I see God reflected in the eyes of those I meet, supporting every form, moving in every act. This movement of Spirit is always revealing more love, more health, more joy, more friends, more great music, more dance, more babies cooing and more puppies playing. Spirit has come to life through me for one purpose alone—to rejoice in life. I put my burdens down and choose to see life as a joyful jubilee.

Hello Walls

I can't say I was born into a happy family. At best, one side had a deep and unabating depression running through it and the other was just straight out, "buck ass crazy".

I tried many therapies—everything from having someone swing a plucked chicken over my head to a super expensive psychologist in Atlanta. By the way, the plucked chicken was a lot less expensive and might have been more effective.

Basically, I've come to accept something that strangely enough my mother would say and that I have heard originated from Abraham Lincoln: "People are about as happy as they make up their minds to be."

It's amazing to me how many of us choose to be unhappy.

Raymond Charles Barker wrote that you cannot cheer up people who are chronically unhappy. They are only happy in their unhappiness. They have been hurt and disappointed by life so much that hurt and disappointment are the only emotions they feel comfortable with and the only ones in which they have faith.

They are only truly happy when they have convinced you that your life should be miserable as well. And if you have the audacity to be happy around them it will irritate them to no end. They don't like happy people: They say they think they're stupid but what they really are is envious.

So, make no attempt to reform them, release them gradually. Barker says make them Christmas card exchange people. I say don't worry about them. You don't have to make any big announcement because they will drift away on their own if you don't give energy to support their misery. Don't feel bad for them, they will soon find someone who will. As they say, there's a bar somewhere playing sad country songs.

My oldest sister, the beauty queen, had a painful first romance. I feel fairly confident that it was also her last. She was a beauty queen after all. During this sad period, she became obsessed with Kitty Wells. Kitty was the queen of country music before Patsy Cline.

My sister wore out a record by Kitty, written by Willie Neilson, entitled, "Hello Walls." It's about a broken-hearted lover coming home to an empty house. Opening up the front door, Kitty sings to the walls, "Hello Walls" and they answer back to her, "Hello, Hello, Hello."

When the inanimate objects in your life start supporting your unhappiness, you know you're in trouble. That's swing a plucked chicken over your head type of stuff (or at least a box of fried chicken from Publix). A tasty dinner with a spiritual healing—a value even at twice the price.

I suppose we all go through periods where we want to sing a sad song for ourselves. When we do, we support our sadness by the energy of our egos and we can't expect much to happen.
Use this prayer to see through your clouds of sadness to the glorious sunshine of God's love.

Affirmative Prayer

I open my spiritual eyes to that which is whole, that which is good and joyful. It is with my spiritual sight that I can see through every cloud of doubt and fear. There may be clouds over my head, but the sun of God's truth still shines brightly. With new vision I look

out onto my world and see
possibilities where once stood
obstructions, health where
once was illness, and
compassion where once was
hostility.

Photo in the Cheese Department

There does seem to be something in our human nature which draws us to the negative side of life. For instance, not being able to pass a car wreck without looking. This curiosity flows not from our spiritual nature but our human nature. We are spirit and dust and it's the dust part of ourselves that gives us most of our trouble.

Freud called it the death wish, or more accurately translated the desire to be unconscious. He said if we didn't have it war would have disappeared long ago. You look at the present opioid epidemic with people killing themselves to be unconscious. There is something to it. So, this tendency to be attracted to the negative is something we should be conscious and mindful of and order our lives in awareness that it is in our nature.

I love cheese of all varieties. I love the expensive stuff you get at Whole Foods. In Atlanta, we lived a block away from Whole Foods. My partner said they had my photo in the back of the cheese department saying not to put out samples if they saw me coming.

But I'm no cheese snob; a good cheddar cheese and a loaf of bread is one of my favorite meals. Yet, if you come to my house you won't find cheese anywhere. I don't trust myself around it. I'm the cheesiest thing allowed in the house. I know better, so I order my life to avoid that propensity. I don't struggle with it; I don't get into a battle with it—that just gives it more energy. I just make the decisions and changes necessary so that I avoid temptation.

If you're hearing a drumbeat of negativity in your life, you may need to take a break from the news, your friends, family or even yourself. Give yourself a few moments of peace each day and repeat this prayer to yourself.

Affirmative Prayer

The presence of Spirit within me blesses everyone I meet, heals everything I touch, and brings gladness into the life of everyone I contact. I am in my right place. I have a right to be here on earth. I am a channel for the goodness of Spirit made manifest. I see the good in others and I bless it. I see the good within myself and I bless it. If I see something other than good, I do my work in thought and prayer to lift my eyes to a better knowing. Through me Spirit looks out onto the world and experiences its love made manifest as my life.

Weirdo in the Bakery

This quote showed up on my laptop, "All evolution is an awakening, a development to a greater possibility, resulting in an unfoldment of inherent possibilities."

That inherent possibility is for happiness, or why else would Spirit have created us if not for the sheer joy of it. When you create joy for yourself and even better for those around you, you have put yourself into the God flow of creation. This is a mighty and wondrous place to be. You can do so in the easiest of ways and it doesn't have to be the big huge gestures. Sometimes it can but it can also be in small human ways which can have a huge impact.

We have a lovely retired minister who comes to our Center. She mentioned that she was turning eighty-five and all her kids were coming to the service the following week. It happened to be a week that I was scheduled to travel away from home for a state conference. Now her only request was that our musical director play special music. She wanted, "Don't Worry, Be Happy."

I thought we should at least get her a sheet cake from the grocery store. On the day that I was to leave, I had thirty minutes before I needed to hit the road. I assumed it would be plenty of time to run by and order a simple cake.

Note to Self: Ordering a cake is never simple.

Not only did it take me twice as long as I had allotted, but I was certain they didn't get the order right. The guy taking the order couldn't have been nicer but I knew I was just as likely to get a bucket of chicken as to get the right cake.

On Sunday, I arrived early and "No" the cake wasn't ready. There was an adorable little lady working at the bakery who promised she'd have it done before I could finish my shopping.

I could just tell that there was something important about the cake for her. I think it was because it was for a minister—particularly a female minister. She mentioned it more than once. Intuitively, I got she was honoring her grandmother.

I didn't say anything. I didn't want to become the weirdo in the bakery. They already keep an eye on me in the cheese department, so I didn't want any more trouble.

When I got back to the bakery, she had finished her masterpiece. With nothing but sugar and butter she had created an entire English rose garden. There were bouquets of roses in the corners, a long-stemmed rose underscoring Rev. Nancy's name and for dramatic effect rose petals floating down the side of the cake.

I was quite taken aback. It almost took my breath. As she boxed it up, she made certain to remind me, "You be sure to wish Rev. Nancy well for us."

Now from some part of her history she was using a memory as a spark to create a new blessing. She had no idea where it was going or what impact it would have. She did her part and released it in Faith. Rev. Nancy's family was so proud of all her honors. They made us stand around the cake as they took countless pictures.

I was still thinking about the cake the next week as I went into the office so I decided I would take one of Rev. Nancy's books to the little lady who had decorated it. I didn't know her name so I just addressed it to the nice lady who decorates cakes on Sunday.

The people working in the bakery immediately knew who I was talking about, Miss Lilly was her name. They were all touched by my gift. I guess bakery workers don't get a lot of praise. You would have thought I had taken them a turkey dinner. They just thought it was the best thing in the world. The manager even gave me a cannoli to take with me.

Sugar and butter were all Miss Lilly had to use to make a blessing, but she did her part and Spirit expanded her love to Rev. Nancy's family, to our congregation and to one happy minister walking back to work with a free cannoli.

It's easier to create a miracle than you think. Do it for yourself and those around you. If you see someone in need, say a prayer for them. You are powerful and God is wanting to awe you with the great good you can do.
Use this prayer:

Affirmative Prayer

The Divine Image in me is what I see in others. All have come from Spirit, created from it plus nothing else. We are one hundred percent God Stuff in the physical plane. In Spirit we live and have our being. From it we draw our inspirations for life. This day I will aspire to live fully, with health, love and prosperity. This day I will see God's good in all others even when they can't see if for themselves. This day I will tread the soil of a new heaven and a new earth.

Love at the Crosswalk

It's always difficult for me to get back into my normal routine after a vacation.

A couple of years ago I was returning from a weekend trip to Charleston which had cost me double my expected expenses when my car decided to blow a gasket on the return home.

While I was gone on my mini-vacation, the washer at home decided to go on strike. Best of all, I found, waiting for me, a letter from my friends at the IRS.

I would have kicked Ernest Holmes in the shins if I could have gotten to him.

Adding to my frustrations was an early morning errand that that took me out of my normal routine. Stuck in school traffic at the neighborhood elementary school I was fuming, but then I saw something that changed my whole outlook.

The traffic was being held up by the school crossing guard. On the side of the street was a little guy. He looked to be in the second or third grade. He wore glasses that were way too big for him and he was carrying a backpack at least as heavy as he was. He was holding a paper in one hand and his mother stood behind him. It was obvious that they were waiting to show something to the crossing guard.

When the guard got to the curb, she bent down to see what the little boy was trying to show her. Whatever was on the paper must have been something really good and hard-worked-for, because after examining it the crossing guard lady hugged the little guy with all her might.

Now here's the thing: standing behind the two of them, the mom was beaming with pride and love.

The crossing guard lady got up that morning, probably with as many frustrations as I had endured, if not more. But she refused to allow her problems to cloud her possibilities. She made a difference, not only for a little kid and his mother, but also for an angry driver stuck in traffic.

When we live with our hearts set on the love mode, we open a world of miracles that can solve any problem from a blown gasket, to a letter from the IRS or even the aspirations of a second grader with glasses far too big and a mom full of hope.

**When we bless the good around us,
our ability to see more of it increases.
Use this prayer to open your eyes to the love and support of Spirit in your life.**

Affirmative Prayer

I know the life of God is the only life there is. That Life is my life now, complete and perfect. That which appears to be less than perfect must come from a misconception on my part. I know that together Spirit and I can overcome any challenge that life puts before me. The world might not know who I am, but God does. So today, I speak and live with courage, faith and conviction that God is love and life is good.

God's Prayer

In my teaching, we believe that Spirit says yes to every request. The problem is that we make a request for a desire—I am ready for my health or my prosperity—then we turn on the news and hear tariffs are threatening the economy. You get to the gym and you think, "I'm the oldest one here; people my age don't get better." Now see - that's a request too, it's just opposite of my desire.

We shouldn't beat ourselves up over this. We're human and we all do it— this is why we call it a practice. It's something we have to work toward.

If we want to experience prosperity, we should strive to put thoughts in our mind that reflect prosperity and do it with more enthusiasm than our habitual thoughts of lack and limitation. Habitual thoughts have energy, but nowhere close to the power of deliberate thoughts. When you catch yourself having habitual and negative thoughts and you can switch over to something positive, you are opening a floodgate of blessings in your life.

All I am and all I choose to express and experience is a co-creative process with the Divine. So, we have to decide what it is that God or the Divine wishes to experience by means of me. Then I have to put my good attention and efforts towards that experience.

In doing so, I can become a cocreator of my good with God. This is why we are here and now is the time to do it. This is the water from the well; if you'll drink, you'll never thirst again.

You don't need another course. You don't need another book or guru. You have all you will ever need to experience all the good that anyone has ever experienced.

We are spirit approved for love, health, prosperity, success and living life with meaning. It first begins in our thinking, "I have what it takes to lead a powerful and dynamic life." It will be good for me and everyone else that I do so.

Knowing this is the nature of my being, I move forward through life in a confident direct manner realizing that what I want is what God knows for me. It's God's prayer for my life. And who am I to say

"NO" to God's prayer. Any idea that you've ever had for your love, health, joy and prosperity, God first had it and Spirit chose to think of you for it.

Do you have children in your life? If you do, you have a wonderful window into Christ Consciousness. For the next couple of weeks, every time you hear the laughter of a child, think back on this prayer.

Affirmative Prayer

Today I allow my soul to be lifted up in song to the Giver of all life and to the joy of living. I allow the brilliance of my soul to shine forth. I seek joy in my life. I look for the goodness of it. I celebrate every time I hear a child's laughter. I send compassion and support when I see an overburdened mom or dad. I bring a lighter mood to those around me. This is good and powerful work and I am grateful for my part in it.

Star Dust

It is no accident at all that you have come to life in this moment. Spirit called you by name from star dust so that you might be here at this time. You have work to do which is important and necessary.

People are quite rightly asking what is going on in our world. Our nation seems to be tearing itself apart. I believe we are going through a period of rebalancing. We are being shown what we don't want so that we can move toward that which is more suited to us. We are being asked to live in a more conscious manner to use our intelligence. Imagine that!

Yes, our weather is changing and the sea level is rising but we have the intelligence to cope. We are not being punished because we drive cars or use air conditioning or produce electricity from coal. We are being shown the consequence of our behavior and we are being given the opportunity to change. Change is possible and it doesn't mean that we a have to go back to living in lack. There is a way to move forward in life in even greater terms. Life is forever expanding.

I've heard that someone asked Mr. Rogers how do we teach our kids to think about all the tragedies and emergences that seem to be happening. He said that when kids see something traumatic on the news, we should point out to them all the people rushing to help.

During a recent natural disaster, I heard of a police officer who died in the line of duty. He was sixty-two years old and he could have retired. His wife told him why don't you stay at home but he replied, "I have work to do." My sister who lives in Louisiana told me that she has a friend, a young man who is raising triplets on his own because his wife tragically died right after their birth—they're only three years old. He went to help with the rescue in one of the hurricanes and the first call he got was to save a single father raising triplets of his own.

Who can deny the hand of God moving through our lives? The question is do we want to stay cowered in our fear and despair or do we want to stand upright and recognize our good and work with it.

One day, soon and very soon, we are going to come together and realize that there is strength in our willingness to help one another. The night may be long but the dawn is breaking. And on that day, we as a people will be strong enough to face any challenge that comes our way.

When we work with the goodness of our souls, we will once again become the light of the world, the hope of mankind.

So now our work is to hold to that vision, to support the goodness we see around us and to walk in faith when we don't see it.

To know it for ourselves, to seek it for our nation and proclaim it for the world.

**A new heaven and a new earth
are what Jesus promised to us. I
believe it is ours to accept
through our love and our joy.
You can create a heaven in your
life by being a source of joy and
harmony. Use this prayer.**

Affirmative Prayer

*As I permit Peace and Love to
flow through my being, mind
and heart, every problem is
released. The way is made clear
filled with joy and harmony. I
dwell in love and peace and I
contemplate them in my
thinking. I release any person,
place or thing which creates ill
ease in my life. I do it with love.
I do what I can to solve the*

problems that challenge me and then I turn them over to Spirit. There is something of God's goodness which wishes to be born through me. I do what I can to bring that goodness to life. Spirit is grateful for me and supports me in every step I take.

Computer Full of Viruses
and
a Car Bellowing Steam

Several years ago, I was one of the organizers for a yearly retreat for the Center for Spiritual Living in Atlanta. The retreat was a big event which required months of planning. Coming home from the successful event, I felt on top of the world. I had met new friends, bonded with old ones and had been inspired by the wisdom of our teachers. Driving home through the torrential rains that Sunday afternoon, I happily hummed the songs I had enjoyed from the guest musicians at service.

Once home, I didn't even allow the discovery that our two doggies had caught fleas while staying with our pet sitter to disturb my new spiritual equilibrium. Wrestling our 4.5-pound pekapoo, who can morph into a Tasmanian devil at the smell of flea soap, I told myself that I was joy riding the universal flow of joy-filled energy.

The next morning, as I went to turn on my laptop and found that it had once again been attacked by a virus, my smile and hum were becoming a little more strained. Driving over to my computer repair shop, my smile became more of a forced grimace when I realized my car AC had suddenly died. Finally, all my newfound enlightenment completely disappeared when I noticed that my car was running hot. Letting loose a blue streak of cussing, I pulled over on the 900 block of Ponce de Leon Place to call a tow truck.

Sitting on the hood of my car, mad with the world, I remembered that at one time, 30 years ago I had actually lived on Ponce De Leon Place. Looking around I discovered, in fact, that my car had died almost directly in front of the house I rented shortly after graduating from college.

At that time our nation was experiencing a terrible recession and jobs, particularly for recent college grads, were difficult to come by. I went to work for a company that provided data transfer for banks. I couldn't have picked a situation that was more poorly suited to my interest. I was convinced that I was stuck in a boring and dead-end position.

During this period, I also learned that my best friend from high school, Claire Moxley, had suddenly died. Claire was funny, smart and tried her best to be a Christian in the most loving sense of the word. She stood over six feet tall and was a dead ringer for Eleanor Roosevelt. She died of heart failure three months into her first job. When I learned of Claire's death, I was devastated. Up until that time, I was a self-confessed atheist and my intellectual honesty could not allow me to believe that my wonderful friend was anything more than dust.

Lying in bed, in my sad little apartment tossing and turning in pain, a thought popped into my head, "Bring a joyful noise unto the Lord." It wasn't a voice and it didn't come with a beam of light, but it was so alien to my consciousness that I knew it had to come from somewhere other than myself. At the time I attributed it to Claire. Now it didn't turn me into a Christian, but it did start me on a journey, one which would allow me to cast off much of the nonsense I had been taught about an angry and judgmental God and lead me to a belief that we are alive to experience God as love and joy.

Sitting in front of my old apartment, I thought that Claire would be proud of the journey I had taken. And I hoped that she would be willing to take some credit for it. And miracle of miracles, that idea made me grateful for a computer full of viruses and a car bellowing steam.

Use this prayer to know that exactly where you are flows a wonderful blessing for you to uncover, accept and become. Say this prayer for yourself.

Affirmative Prayer

Today the Truth leads me into the possession of everything necessary to my well-being. Everything is made new and I expect and accept only good. I let go of any idea or conclusion that no longer serves me. I only entertain those ideas which support my greater living. Spirit is forever evolving, so I know that I am inspired to think in greater terms: to have a family that supports and encourages me, to have a wonderful set of friends who remind me to play, to dance and not take myself so seriously, to have meaningful work, and to be supported financially so that I can live generously for myself and those around me.

One Bitterly Cold Night

I think it was Rumi who said it is better to sit at the temple door and beg alms than work without joy.

After I got out of college, I bounced around jobs some before settling into waiting tables. I knew it wasn't a good choice for me, so I went back to school to study international economics. Not that I had any interest in International Economics but I thought knowing how to make money had to be a good thing.

One day, I got to campus early to study for a test. I saw a notice on a bulletin board about an internship for our local Congressman in DC. To apply you had to write three essays. Instead of studying, I wrote out the application.

Months later I received my acceptance. Within just moments of reading the letter I made the decision to move to DC. All of my friends were opposed to the idea, but I knew it was my one chance out and I was determined to make the most of it. I loved Washington and the Congressman's office but unfortunately, they had recommended an apartment in the suburbs in an old run-down furnished apartment. It wasn't my idea of a new life.

To get to the apartment required that I take the subway to the end of the line at Pentagon Station and then transfer onto a bus. The busses stopped running early so I had to leave my new friends partying while I made the long trek back to a dusty and musty apartment. On a bitterly cold night, I ran up from the stairs of the subway to see my bus pulling out in the frigid and lonely January night. The next bus wouldn't arrive for an hour.

Sitting in the desolate parking lot, I was determined to stew in my frustration. I had just settled into my misery when I noticed, far in the distance, a lone figure coming up the Metro escalator. As soon as I saw her in the huge parking lot, I knew without a doubt she was coming to my stop.

As much as I was determined not to talk, my new bench mate was determined that we would. Like me she had just moved to DC. Her home was Ethiopia which had just been taken over by a communist government. In her previous life, she had owned an art gallery and she had specialized in religious icons. The Ethiopian Christian church is the oldest Christian branch and some of her icons were hundreds of years old. The communists had forced her to flee so she left with some of her most valuable pieces. The plan had been to sell the icons in DC where she had heard there was a wealthy African American community and then pay for her teenagers to come to join her.

Unfortunately, once in the states, she realized that Americans didn't consider religious icons as African art. After a couple of months trying, she had resorted to working at fast food restaurants in downtown DC.

She was neither bitter nor depressed. She was greatly impressed with the organization of the restaurants and she worked hard. She told me that she also enjoyed counseling the young people she worked with. "I do it," she said, "because I'm praying that someone is spending time with my kids, keeping them on the right path."

That was a woman working in faith. She could have been angry and hostile. Instead she was doing what was right before her to do, placing faith in the goodness of God.

Today have faith that you are loved by God and that you are right where you need to be. Use this prayer when you want to know that right where you are Spirit can provide the blessings you need to experience all the good of life.

Affirmative Prayer

I listen with complete faith and trust to the voice of Love guiding me today. I accept the abundant good that flows easily and freely to me. I know the love I express blesses all. Love heals every condition. I am immersed in it. Today I commune with Spirit. I see the Divine Presence in my life.

*Through my experience I
realize its beauty and I am
consciously aware of its love.*

Tow Truck Guy Heaven

Now one of the things we often do is discount those things which come naturally to us. We all have something which comes to us easily. It is our gift from Spirit and ours to develop and give back to the world. It's up to us to put the energy into it and to make the most of it.

Don't discount it. Often times we think because we have something that comes easily to us that it comes easily to everyone. This isn't true.

Hopefully, we don't have this too much anymore, but at one time you used to hear women say, "I'm just a mom" as if raising the next generation was something to be discounted or that anyone could do it.

If you are a parent of a child who's happy and productive, and if your home is the sort of home where your kid's friends feel comfortable, then you are doing great and important work. It will pay dividends.

I think it was Jackie Onassis who said if you haven't raised your kids well it doesn't matter what else you have done in life.

It takes a lot of sacrifice of time and energy to raise a happy and healthy kid. At some point in the process your heart is going to be broken.

I had an uncle who worked as a mechanic and drove a tow truck at night. He put his daughter through three years of college when she decided to switch to nursing. When she told him she was leaving college she thought he would be upset.

Instead, he told her that it was his job to pay for her education, and hers to study for it.

My aunts thought he was the biggest fool that ever walked the earth. "Make her finish her college," they told him or at least make her pay for the nursing. "Tell her to get a job at Walmart," they insisted. "It's the only way she would learn."

In the end they were all wrong. She ended up being quite successful running one of the biggest prenatal hospital departments in Georgia.

The last time I visited him she had bought him a trailer on lake Sinclair. It was only a single wide, but he could not have been prouder. She had a big screen porch built on the front with a TV and even a mini fridge. Having a little refrigerator next to his lazy boy was just the damnedest thing he thought. He loved fishing so she bought him a boat and built him a pier. He was in tow truck guy heaven.

He had been no fool. He did his job on the tow truck but he also did his work in consciousness. He held to the vision that his daughter was going to be successful and productive.

See, the aunts wanted to put her to work to learn her lesson, but instead he inspired her through his vision of her. She worked a lot harder trying to live up to his vision than she would have ever worked learning a hard lesson at Walmart.

I may not be able to see how my good can come to me, but God does. We look too far away for our good. Tow truck guy heaven is close by with a comfortable chair on the porch, a great view and something cold to drink. Use this prayer when you want to open
your eyes to the heaven around you.

Affirmative Prayer

I expect every good thing to come to me, everything worthy of my soul. My destiny and destination are certain. The Kingdom of Heaven is at hand. The Perfection of God flows through my life. It dissipates all the obstructions of life transforming all confusion into love and beauty. I have absolute faith in the principle of life and the law of love. I permit love in its freedom to express through me, to radiate from me.

The Best Insurance Policy

I love reading a good biography. One curious thing I've noticed from my reading is that people with large amounts of money often end up being treated very poorly at the end of their lives. When they did an autopsy of Howard Hughes, they found syringe needles broken off in his body. His story is not unique. There was suspicion that Doris Duke was killed by her butler while he wore her gowns and jewelry. Doris was so disgusted by the greed of the world that she said when she died, she hoped they would dump her in the deep sea in the middle of a shark feeding frenzy.

So, if money isn't enough to ensure a comfortable end, what is?

My mom had a best friend named Mrs. King. She would always tell my mom, "Helen, see the best in others, and everything will work out."

Mrs. King had been a child bride, raised five kids, widowed early and in her eighties ran to become mayor of her small town. She won her election and just happened to be the oldest person in the nation elected to office for that election cycle. She was interviewed on national news by Matt Lauer who got her age wrong. She scolded him on national TV and from then on got a yearly birthday card from him. As she became more infirm, her family, friends and community turned out in droves to help. People could not do enough for the woman who had seen and reflected the best of themselves.

The best insurance policy can't be bought; it just comes from our willingness to see God reflected back to us in the eyes of those surrounding us.

It may seem over simplistic but being a loving person is one of the most powerful statements you can make in life. Be loving to yourself and those in your life. See yourself as God sees you— courageously kind, bravely generous and boldly loving. Use this prayer.

Affirmative Prayer

There is a Power in which all things are possible. The Power of Mind is right where I am. I use It for good with every thought. I let go of any idea of less than or woundedness. They are infantile ideas and I have played with them long enough. As a spiritual adult I lift my eyes to a better knowing: that I am one with God, that God is good. I tread the soil of the earth so that I may proclaim my oneness with God through joy, love and laughter. Nothing is too hard for God and there is nothing too good for me.

A Jack and Coke with Half a Valium

My mother was not your typical mother. While my friends went home to find afternoon snack, I was as likely to be met with a request for a cigarette, and a jack and coke with half a valium. My mom always thought it was a sign of good breeding to only take half of a valium like a lady ordering a glass of sherry at a cocktail bar. If nothing else my teenage years skilled me in the technique of splitting pills.

It took me a long time to come to peace with my Mom and to appreciate what she was able to give and share.

One thing which I'm sure she didn't realize she was teaching me was how dramatically you can change the direction of your life. Within just a period of eighteen months Mom went from Church of God mom while my dad was alive, to honkey tonk mom after he had died.

It was quite the journey. Now it didn't happen immediately; for a good eighteen months she wallowed in depression, which was sort of surprising since she had heretofore never really had much nice to say about Dad.

But within a year and a half of his passing, she left the Church of God to find meaning and comfort in Jack Daniels, the lounge at the Disabled American Veterans (from which she was later to be barred for life, but that's another story altogether) and Conway Twitty.

She sort of became obsessed with Conway, with his shellacked black hair and pastel blue leisure suits. His backup singers were named the Twitty Birds—I would have gladly shot them all. His biggest hit, "Hello Darling," became the anthem of her new-found freedom.

While in my adulthood, I did develop an over appreciation for Jack Daniels, I never warmed to Conway. Although I did have to admit that my mom was much easier to live with after she discovered his crooning. I think she had a lot more fun, explored life and came more into her own. She was extremely intelligent; if given the opportunity she would have been a brilliant lawyer.

She was loyal to friends and brutally honest, a quality friends greatly valued, while family members found it a bit taxing. It was sort of like blue cheese dressing; a little of it went a long way and if you got too much of it you could go off of it for a while.

She was bitingly funny. Ninety-nine percent of the stuff she said I can't share with you. I think she crossed over to true comedy genius with her famous retort to my father's driving. "Sammy," she would yell, "your driving is making me so nervous my ass can eat soggy soda crackers." I spent years in different counseling and psychology offices trying to work out the physiological and psychological implications of that one.

Right before my father died, my parents purchased one of the spookiest houses you could have ever imagined. I can envision the real estate flyer describing a haunted house, mass murder included, with poltergeist thrown in for free.

I never learned what happened in the house but it wasn't good. It was large and built in the shape of an "L". You could never be sure there wasn't someone at the other end of it. Two of the bedrooms had doors that went outside. There were constant sounds and bumps through the night. Sometimes you could swear you heard a door open or a voice only to find an empty room.

When they purchased the house there were five of us in the family. Within a year after Dad had died it was just the two of us. Quite naturally, she was concerned about being in a huge house with just me, so she inquired about having an alarm system installed.

The company she called sent a young man out to explain the system to her. He told her that in the dead of the night, while she was peacefully sleeping, if someone came along and took a brick and smashed it through her bedroom window the 3000 KX system would turn on all the lights and set off a siren in the attic loud enough to be heard a block away. For added results it would also automatically dial the phone for the police.

"Mister," she told him, "If I am sleeping peacefully one night and someone takes a brick and smashes it through my bedroom window and a siren goes off and the lights come on you might as well have the phone call the mortuary because they'll find me dead with a heart attack."

Sometimes we all wake up to bumps in the night which can scare us. Use this prayer to release fear and to know that love is the greatest power in your life.

Affirmative Prayer

Greater than fear is Love. It can accomplish all things through the Inner Light of that faith which fills my Being with a Powerful Presence. So today, I let go of every thought which is not loving to those around me and particularly to myself. I realize that sometimes I struggle and give in to the lessor part of myself. It's not always easy being human, but starting today I am going to love myself completely and totally. I will whisper sweet words of encouragement to myself. I will remind myself that as I know better I do better. So today, I will aspire to the best part of myself. I will choose to see that inspiration in others. I will lift my eyes up to a better knowing for myself, my world and my God.

Sweet Dreams of You

Now mom didn't always love me in the way I needed, but she loved me in the way she could. The bottom line is that's all you can ask of anyone. For a long time now, I've tried to see her as a fellow traveler on life's journey. It was very healing for me to find a photo of her in her teens. She was quite the beauty and so hopeful. That's the idea of her to which I cling. Wherever she might be on her journey, I like to think my decision to think better of her helps lighten her load. I certainly know it helps lighten mine. When bad memories come up for me about her, and even though she has been gone from my life for over twenty years now they still do, I try to think back on happy times.

I think the times she most loved was when I was in my thirties working in DC. I would come down for the Christmas holidays and go out to her favorite juke joint—the Veterans of Foreign Wars' lounge (VFW).

She and her husband John found the VFW after they were barred for life from the Disabled American Veteran's bar (DAV). Supposedly, because I don't have confidence that we ever got the total truth of the story, Mom was voicing an opinion when a man challenged her. John got involved and at some point, the man went to take a swing at him. Mom knocked the assailant out cold with an empty Jack Daniels bottle. Conway Twitty would have been so proud. She swore the bottle was full, but I know better. She would have never risked spilling that much good liquor.

It all worked out for the better because the VFW lounge was actually kind of a nice place. At the piano they had an entertainer who sounded for all the world like Patsy Cline. Mom would show me off to her friends as her son who worked for the Congressman. I think as proud of me as she was then, she would be even prouder of me now. I'm grateful that I've had this journey.

So, if I think of a time when she wasn't very loving toward me, I try to tell myself she knows better now. And then I replace that memory with a vison of her waiting for me surrounded by all her friends at the VFW lounge where there are twinkling Christmas lights and cutouts of Santa decorating the walls and lyrics of "Sweet Dreams" floating over the crowd.

Raymond Charles Barker wrote, "Yesterday ended last night and today begins when I choose to have a better Idea for myself." Say this prayer when you want to release negative memories.

Affirmative Prayer

Today is a new day and I am feeling good. The Spirit of God has brought me to life so that I might experience all the love and laughter life has to offer. If there is something in my past holding me back from my best experience, I let it go. Today, I proclaim the good news of my soul that I am here to bring God's Sweet Dreams to life. God won't have it any other

*way and neither will I. This is
my truth and I release it to the
mind of God to return to me
multiplied abundantly.*

Holidays with a Burst Pipe

Last year a friend was feeling a bit down because right before the holidays a pipe burst in her kitchen ruining her flooring and cabinets. Even with insurance it took all her holiday savings to get her kitchen back to a usable state.

My friend is one of those people who invites all the strays to her house for the holidays. Out of a tiny kitchen that is little bigger than a closet, she prepares holiday meals for sometimes up to forty people.

Her biggest concern with the coming season was that she wouldn't have the money to buy her college-age son his Christmas request (Polo shirts) or to get a tree large enough to match their Christmas tradition.

Overriding all of this was the worry that her son might find out that she was running short on money. With no kitchen and little funds, she was still determined to enjoy the Holiday as best she could.

The week before he was due to arrive from college, she had made a trip to the mall to price a Polo shirt. She quickly realized that her budget and Ralph Lauren were operating in two separate financial worlds. Leaving the mall, she happened to pass a Goodwill store. Thinking that she might pick up some kitchen items that had been ruined in her flood, she stopped in. Just on a lark she thought she would look through the men's clothing and to her great surprise she came across an entire batch of gently used Polo shirts. It was as if Ralph himself had cleaned out his closet for the holidays. For less than the cost of one shirt at the Mall, she walked away with a bag full.

Still with no tree, she waited for her son to arrive home. Taking one look at his mom's kitchen floor, he decided that he would spend his holidays putting in a tile floor for her. For the next several days he worked around the clock to get the floor installed. By the time he was finished it was only the day before Christmas Eve.

With no time left to stall, she went with her son to go buy a tree. Pulling up at the neighborhood lot they noticed a sign on the gate, "I've gone back home to North Carolina to spend the holidays with my family. All the trees are free. Merry

Christmas to All." My friend and her son hauled back to her condo a tree that would have cost them well over a hundred dollars just a few days earlier.

It's easy to think we've got to make things happen, but sometimes all we have to do is to keep the right frame of mind and allow our good to come to us.

Spirit loves a party. When was the last time you danced? After saying this prayer, put a happy song on and move your feet for a bit. Even if you have to sit down to do it. God loves a good time and there's no reason you can't have one in your life.

Affirmative Prayer

There are no impossibilities today. With God there is the eternal evolution of a greater good, greater love and greater health. I release any idea that I have to live in lack or limitation. I am here to laugh, play and dance with family and friends. To see the good in my life and to proclaim it for others. To be awed with the support and love that God has for me.

Singing Carols

While my mother was still alive, I always worried how I would spend my Christmases after she died. The last several Christmases of my mom's life were particularly fun. My two youngest sisters had little ones and Mom's house was always full of people coming and going. Mom would spend weeks cooking different cakes and cookies, and my stepdad always insured there was a bottle of something around the place.

My concerns about being alone on the holidays were a little justified. I had never had a long-term relationship and I didn't think our family would continue getting together without mom. The first Christmas after her death, I went to a friend's whose large Catholic family started celebrating the holiday a week before, so it was just one long party for them.

The next year I was in a relationship and so being alone on the holidays was never a concern.

And the truth of the matter is that I'm now surrounded by more people during the holidays than ever. St. Augustine is known worldwide for its holiday lights. At our church we begin planning for the season months in advance. We have two holiday drives, one for kids in need and the other for older residents at an assisted living facility.

We never have to decorate the auditorium because our stage is filled with gift bags and bicycles. A week before Christmas, we rent one of the tourist buses downtown and we fill it up with our community. We get off in the middle of Constitution Plaza and sing carols to the tourists. Our music director plays his accordion, and before we pile back on the bus, we have a huge crowd singing with us.

On Christmas Eve we have a candle lighting service at the church. Afterwards, we drive downtown to have drinks at an old historic hotel in St. Augustine. It turns out to be a magical night.

On Christmas day, a group of us go to the assisted living facility to hand out presents and to sing more carols. We then go back to my house for a potluck.

Christmas night friends from out of town arrive and for the next several days we'll spend the afternoons watching all the big releases at the movies. It makes for a perfect holiday season, and sometimes I just have to wonder that at one time I was afraid that I would be alone.

Fear, worry and old conclusions about ourselves and our lives can block off any access we have to the goodness of life. Release any limiting idea you have for yourself or your life. Use this prayer.

Affirmative Prayer

There is only one Divine Mind and that Mind is now operating in my life. This intelligence supports the best for my life. I let go of every false idea I have ever accepted as my own. They are shadows of the truth. As I accept this reality in my life, the full potential of the Universe will be revealed to me. New horizons open up for me, new ideas flow to me and a better world is revealed. I am saying "Yes" to it all. I am grateful for these empowered ideas and I now release them to return to me multiplied.

Vicks VapoRub

My teacher used to say that the thing that made you sick is the only thing that can heal you. In other words, it's your thinking that made you ill and it will be your thinking that will make you well. Most certainly, your estimation of the possibility for your healing will determine the length of your illness.

This fact was proved to me long before I ever heard of Religious Science. The summer I graduated university the nation was in the midst of a recession. With few job prospects for a degree in psychology, I moved back home to Macon (never a good idea) to spend a miserably hot and humid summer.

Shortly after I had adjusted myself to my mother's new hobby room, which at one time had been my bedroom, I woke up to a bad case of laryngitis. I could barely speak above a whisper. For the next two weeks I endured all of my mother's home remedies; hot tea with honey and lemons was the most pleasant. With no improvement, I was soon subjected to every cure she heard from her sisters to her hair dresser. Having to sleep with Vicks VapoRub on the soles of my feet was a particularly medieval one.

Still with no improvement, my Mom forced me to go to the family doctor. After a week of his attention I was still speaking in a whisper and was sent off to a specialist. A week with the specialist offered no better results. Finally, I was given an appointment with what was considered the best specialist in Macon. That distinction alone should have given me pause.

The next morning, I found myself sitting in a hospital gown waiting for the good doctor. The extra-large gown didn't quite fit me, so the nurse went to announce to the entire nurse's station that they had a big one, "who liked his momma's biscuits too much." I wanted to bang my head against the examining room wall.

When the doctor finally breezed in, he barely acknowledged my presence before wrapping my tongue in gauze and yanking it to the very root. Turning his back to me, he pronounced to the dutiful nurse taking notes that I had a paralyzed larynx and would never speak normally again. When I asked him about possible treatments, he suggested that I learn sign language as he finished his dictations.

I went home devastated. I had no reason to doubt him. He certainly seemed confident in his diagnosis. My future now seemed completely bleak and without potential.

For a couple of weeks, I stayed hibernating in my room. Finally, my older sister, who lived in Atlanta, made an appointment for me to see a specialist at Emory.

By this point, I had no hope left of recovery, but all that turned around with the new doctor. I can't remember his name but he was full of enthusiasm and hope. He looked at my throat and told me I had a bad case of post nasal drip aggravated by the heat and humidity of Macon. With the right medications he assured me I would be talking within the week.

Now here's the interesting point of the story, it didn't take a week; in fact, I was talking in my normal voice within twenty-four hours. Whatever other medications the doctor from Emory gave me, he also gave me the hope that I could be cured. And it was that idea which allowed me, helped no doubt by the medications, to cure myself in record time.

Louise Hay wrote, "Love yourself, heal your life." Love points us in the direction of our healing. This is a great prayer when you need a healing of love in your life.

Affirmative Prayer

Love makes my way clear. It guides me in an ever-widening experience of living. My every thought and act are an expression of this goodness. I look out onto my world and I see evidence of the power of love. I give love and I receive it in ever expanding ways. I love myself and I praise myself. I look out in the world and seek expressions of love. When I see acts of love, I give gratitude for them, I bless them. I know they are the very presence of God making itself manifest in my life, empowering me, encouraging me. This is my truth and I am grateful for it.

Kale Smoothie

There is something of Spirit that wishes to be birthed in our lives. We are needed and necessary to bring those dreams to reality. Without us the dream of Spirit will not happen. And the world and life will be less for it. We are the midwife to the Spirit of God in the physical plane—just that important—just that valued.

Our goal is to keep our attention on our best possibilities. When fears and doubts pop up in our thinking, set them aside and lift up our eyes unto the hills of our better knowing.

So, right now my best possibility is that I should be eating healthier and getting more greens in my system. I decided that a good way to do that was with a kale smoothie each morning.

Day two of that program my intention changed from having a kale smoothie to having a kale smoothie that tastes good. So, I set the intention that I will make a good tasting kale smoothie. I see myself at the blender with the bag of kale, preparing the smoothie, enjoying the smoothie.

That imagery sets up a vibration. The more I can hold on to the vibration the stronger it will get and the greater the possibility will be that I will come up with a recipe for a good tasting Kale smoothie.

When we hold an intention in our thinking, we'll start getting little fireflies of ideas—just twinkling in the dark. Play with them, honor them and give gratitude for them. You may get an idea like "I'll try the smoothie with a mango!"

You may be reading on the bag of kale and think, now wait a minute I can also sauté it with a little olive oil and garlic. That will show Kale who's the boss.

Or, I'm at the grocery store and it suddenly dawns on me I don't have to have kale at all. I can get a cantaloupe.

Okay, so I have the idea which is basically to eat healthier. That's the big idea. Kale is the manifestation of that desire on which I have chosen to focus. I can narrow the path of how my good can come to me but Spirit has all of creation to get my blessings to me.

By my setting my intention, I have created a vibration of greater health. By holding on to it, by not getting discouraged, it will reflect back to me as an experience that matches the vibration of the original intentions. Kale or not, but always for my good.

Say this prayer when you want to feel empowered by Spirit. When you want to know that with God's help you can overcome any challenge that can ever confront you.
Even if it seems as unsurmountable as creating a good tasting kale smoothie.

Affirmative Prayer

I know my good is at hand. I see this good in persons, places and things. Nothing but goodness can come from me and return to me. I let go of every thought of lack or limitation. They only have the power that I give them and I now cut the energetic cord that has sustained them. I look out on the world and see a bounty of joy and love. I step up to take my share. Spirit called me forth from star dust to be here. Here today, I release any idea that I must live in lack and limitation. I am open and grateful for the full measure of God's blessing in my life.

Greater Possibilities

Now, here's something to try. Take your idea for a better life and link it with a memory when you felt really loved and supported.

The imagery is of Moses in the basket of reeds. Moses represents our desires; the basket represents loving and supportive memories. When we set them afloat on the river of consciousness amazing things can happen.

Strong held memories both good and bad have created deep patterns in our thinking. Those patterns are reservoirs for strong emotions. When we link our desires with deep emotions, we create powerful intentions. In doing this we have created a mental picture of the thing desired. This is a very powerful spiritual tool.

It's never a matter of trying to convince God that we deserve our good. God is already convinced. We're the ones that need convincing. So, I take my desire for a good tasting kale smoothie and I link it with my memory of a loving aunt who used to slip me money when I was a broke college student. I throw then both into consciousness.

In mind that idea will magnetize events that will reflect back to me those emotions and feelings of my intention.

That will happen if I don't set up roadblocks of negativity and morbidity which we love to do.

The whole crux of our lives is where we are focusing our attention: Is it on the good of life or the negative? On our greater possibilities or our loss and disappointments?

Use this prayer if you're experiencing any lack in your life. It may be lack of prosperity or health, energy or love. Spirit has never experienced any form of lack or limitation and you don't need it either. Like Moses in the weeds you are supported and safe.

Affirmative Prayer

My Divine birthright is freedom and eternal goodness. Life gives according to my faith. I lift up my spirit and listen to the song of my Soul. I have absolute faith in the Principle of Life and the Law of Love. I permit Love in its freedom to express through me to radiate from me. Boldly I express my desires. All that God has is mine. I draw from my spiritual source all that I need to live joyously in love, prosperity and health.

Chunky Monkey

The other day I got up early so I could take the dogs out for a walk before the heat and bugs got their start. You would think taking two dogs for a walk would be easy but there is a whole diplomacy involved in the process. One of our dogs, Sadie, walks fast, so she goes out first. The other one, Maddie, is more of a stroller than a walker. So, after taking Sadie for a lap around the neighborhood, I go back home to get Maddie for a more leisurely sojourn. Getting a prisoner out of North Korea would be easier.

Maddie, the Sheltie, we got two years ago. Her previous owner had just left her in a cage and fed her. She became very overweight, but with a smart diet and lots of encouragement she's lost a good bit of her weight. We also encourage her to go on walks. She loves her food—the walks she only tolerates.

During one of our walks, we were met by a little German lady who likes to pet the two of them. While she was leaning down scratching Maddie's side, she looked up to me and remarked, "Why she's a little Chunky Monkey."

Now, I'm of the school, "I can talk bad about my family, but I don't need anybody's help." Since Maddie really doesn't understand English I was thinking, "No harm no foul."

Then she looked up at me patted me on my stomach and said, "Well you're a Chunky Monkey too."

For a moment I was ten seconds away from, as one of my sisters would say, opening up a family sized can of Whoop-Ass on her. Fortunately, as often has happened in my life, my humor came to the rescue. I don't remember what I said but it was enough to excuse myself and carry on with my walk.

I would like to say that I didn't let it bother me but the truth of the matter is that I didn't wake up that morning hoping to be called a chunky monkey. It really wasn't the look I was going for when I dressed.

So, I began to think how can I turn this from a negative into a positive? Because after all this little lady never in the world would have wanted me to feel bad or hurt. Then I thought, well Ben & Jerry's has made a million dollars selling Chunky Monkey so if I'm a chunky monkey it has to come with a million dollars of blessings for my life.

So, here's the challenge. Can I release my negative thoughts long enough so I can move into my power? Am I strong enough to make the tweaks to my thinking that will allow me to move to thoughts which are life affirming? If I can, then I am well on my way to co-creating heaven on earth. I will have done my part, then it's up to Spirit to do Its.

This is a great prayer to release any negativity. Say it on a beautiful day when you can go outside, lean against a tree and listen to the birds.

Affirmative Prayer

Divine Intelligence guides me. Joy flows into my thought and work. Peace and harmony attend everything I do. Love is ever present. I keep my mind, thought and expectations open to new experiences, to happier events, to a more complete self-expression. My eyes are open to the breadth, height and depth of that Life which is God's life. Today, I will feel this Presence as a living reality.

This Day in Paradise

There are situations in life you can't laugh your way out of. I sometimes think my fellow New Thought ministers describe life as a place where the unicorns run free and cotton candy grows wild. Unfortunately, there is pain in life and there are dark paths that we must all tread.

I have a friend who has a terrible cancer. His partner called me early one Friday to tell me that they were running out of pain medications and the insurance wouldn't cover any more. They desperately needed a new prescription and the only place to go was the public hospital. From where they live it takes more than an hour to get to the hospital and then the wait to see the doctor can easily take several hours.

When I got off the phone, I started doing prayers. I envisioned everything lining up: the doctors, the insurance and the pharmacy.

The next time I talked to him he told me that on his first try he had been able to get a doctor on the phone. Looking over the records, the doctor realized that she could switch the prescription to morphine and the insurance would pay for as much of it as he needed.

Then the question became how do I move forward in my prayers for my friend? If I'm being totally honest, my human side doesn't see him being healed. How can I pray in integrity?

Well, I pray for his comfort, peace and ease. I pray for his healing, as best as I can see it. We are told to look a condition squarely in the face, yet still know the truth.

I also pray for divine right order. See, I don't know all that Spirt knows, but what I know of God is that It is loving and compassionate. So there has to be a loving and compassionate answer.

When I turn to that thought, I see my friend in a fluffy house coat sipping tea in their garden full of birds. In that moment he is healed, and if he can be healed for one moment, he can be healed for eternity.

When Jesus was on the cross, beaten to an inch of his life, crowned with thorns, and rejected by his followers and even God, the thief next to him cried out. Jesus said, "This day I'll meet you in paradise." It's a remarkable statement. I will be in paradise and you will join me. In his pain and rejection, Jesus still was able to lift his eyes to a better knowing. It would have been human for him to just stay focused on his own pain but he chose to be about his Father's work. In that moment, he was free.

Sometimes, I hate to say, life can knock us on our rears. And sometimes on our rears is exactly where we need to be to get a different viewpoint. Say this prayer when you need to dust yourself off and start over again.

Affirmative Prayer

No harm can come to me because I dwell in the secret place of the Most High. I abide under the protection of the Almighty. I know that Life gives to me according to my faith. Today I elevate my faith and mind. I engage Spirit as It flows through me with inspiration. I have absolute faith in the Principle of Life and the Law of Love. I permit Love to express through me, to radiate from me, to heal, bless and prosper.

One Chunky Monkey on the Loose!

When they nailed him to the cross, the world thought they were rid of Jesus. They thought they could throw him in a tomb and be done with him, but the power and compassion in his soul would not be held back.

As you are reading this, you may have allowed the world to put you in a tomb.

You may have allowed the world to roll a stone of lack and limitation, of woundedness and victimhood over the doorway of your dreams.

But you can look at any stone and say mountain be moved for God's dreams must breathe the air of life.

I may have been down, I may have been out, but I am taking back my power. I am proclaiming the good news of my soul. I am lifting up my eyes and seeing heaven on earth for myself and those around me.

See, the world may have discounted you. The world may have given up on you and the world may have not seen the best of you.

At times you might have even given up on yourself but God never did. So go tell it to the mountains. You haven't seen anything yet because Spirit and I have work to do. Stone, roll back. Spirit and I are bursting out because there is one chunky monkey on the loose!

This is a prayer to elevate our faith. We only need the faith of a mustard seed. How much faith is that? The faith it takes to do the prayer in the first place. God is closer than your next breath, and this prayer will help you see and feel that reality.

Affirmative Prayer

Today, I consciously let go of every discord. I drop all sense of lack or limitation from my thought. I release every belief I have ever had in fear. Supporting me is the potential of the Universe. New horizons will open for me, new ideas will flow to me and a better world will be revealed. The

Divine Intelligence within me is transcendent of all previous experiences. This right knowing in me is making everything new in my life.

Spirituality for the Slothful

I was listening to a friend describing his new Spiritual practice. It all sounded rather painful. The entire time I was listening I kept thinking, "Why don't you just join the Army?"

Some of us think we have to spend hours in a painful practice when all we really need to do is recognize the love of God in the sunrise, a child's laughter, a great meal or when we're just feeling really good. I truly believe the Universe was created for nothing more than the sheer joy of it. And if this is the case then certainly, we are able to reach out to the Creator in joy.

I've always liked the fact that the first miracle Jesus performed was the changing of the water into wine.

In other words, he produced his first miracle when he was having a good time. Ernest Holmes wrote that we look too far away for our good. We are never any closer to God than when we're really enjoying our lives.

So, I would like to propose a Spirituality for the Slothful. It is something very easy and simple that anyone can manage. Tomorrow when you wake up just spend a few moments before you get out of bed awakening the Divine Dream within yourself. Think of those things that make you feel more alive. Imagine how your life could reflect more of the Divine Pattern of Joy.

As you go through your day set signals to remind yourself of this

Divine Dream and reflect on what part of your day has seemed Divine.

The sloth has been criticized for being lazy and unproductive. Scientists tell us that at one time it was a land-dwelling mammal and very large. At some point, the sloth decided to give up the rat race and ascend to the canopy of trees. There it hangs by his claws safely above the danger of the jungle, gently resting on his back munching on the leaves overhead.

I imagine him meditating on the sunlight gently filtering through the tree limbs overhead, and I wonder what the sloth thinks about? I would like to think it's contemplating this wonderful Universe of ours and the Glory of God.

Just as the sloth sees the goodness of God in the sun's light filtered through the jungle canopy, know that the love of God filters through your thinking. Post this prayer right at your front door. When you step out say to yourself:

Affirmative Prayer

I know my good is at hand. I see this good in persons, places and things. Nothing but goodness can come from me and return to me. Love makes my way clear. It guides me in an ever-widening experience of living. My every thought and act are an expression of this goodness. I know my presence

upholds and blesses everyone I contact.
A healing power goes forth from me.
Today I will help everyone I meet.

Swallow a Bug

This past week, I was asked to do a sunrise memorial service on the beach. Normally, I absolutely refuse to do any kind of service on the beach. The beach is a lovely place for laying in the sun, playing in the water and volleyball. It is no place for a ceremony. It's loud—most people forget that and there's no volume switch on it. It's sandy, it's buggy and there is this thing called the tide which people planning ceremonies always seem to forget. While they may ask everyone to dress casually, the minister is expected to dress a little nicer. So, there I am in my dress shoes looking like Nixon walking on the beach.

I had agreed to do this service because I felt such love and pain coming from this family. I wanted to help in any way I could. Their young adult child had been murdered and abandoned in the desert. The family wasn't religious and didn't want prayers, so it was a difficult talk. My prayer partner helped me write it and I thought we had done a lovely job. At the service there was no sound system and it turned out to be a large crowd. There were probably over 100 people there so I was really having to speak loudly. Right in the middle of the talk, a bug flew straight into my mouth. Now, I had a choice—either swallow the bug, or spit it out in front of this family who is already in desperate pain. So, I swallowed the bug.

Driving home, I was emotionally drained, my clothes were soaked through with sweat and I was covered in sand. Getting into an extremely hot car, I noticed that someone that I really don't know had posted something political on Facebook that didn't set well with me. It might have been because I was suffering from bug indigestion, but I wasn't in the mood.

Normally, I just unfollow anyone who upsets me but I had found her post so personal and egregious that I not only unfriended her but I let her know I was doing it. She wrote back a long, thoughtful reply. I responded that I didn't want to get into a political argument, I was on my way home to gargle with disinfectant. After that she didn't write back. I think she quite correctly realized that she was dealing with someone with issues.

I got home and called my prayer partner who's going through chemo. I wanted to let her know how the memorial had gone and how grateful I was for her help. I didn't bring up the Facebook incident because she has enough turmoil in her life.

After we were finished talking about the funeral, she began to tell me about a prayer shawl she had received from a minister friend of ours. The shawl came with affirmations for healing. She read some of them to me. She said that when she wore the shawl, she could feel the love coming from it.

I knew the minister of the Church who had knitted the shawl. I hadn't been in touch with her for a long time. I sent her a note letting her know how much her show of love had meant to our friend.

She was so grateful hearing from me because she said they don't always hear that the shawls are being used. Before she hung up, she called me by a nickname that only she uses for me: Southern Comfort.

A few weeks ago, I got called a Chunky Monkey, so I'm seeing a food and drink trend going on here. I guess Southern Comfort is an improvement over being called a bowl of ice cream.

Proclaim your good for yourself, regardless of what the world is telling you. The next time you're caught in a rain storm, stand for a moment in the rain and say: From the storehouse of Infinite Good, my blessings rain down. Your neighbors will think you're crazy, but it's a small price to pay.

Affirmative Prayer

I see God everywhere and where God is no evil endures. Today ideas from the Divine Mind will make my life a perfect expression of the limitless bounty. From the storehouse of Infinite Good, my blessings will rain down. Within me is limitless faith in the Presence of Good. It flows into my world of thought and action, bringing peace and harmony to my life.

Southern Comfort

When I first came to New Thought Spirituality it seemed to me that the gist of it was that if we only got our thinking in line our lives would unfold naturally and beautifully. I still believe that is true. I also think we have another task which is to allow the goodness of Spirit to flow through our lives to those around us. Not to be a martyr but through our joy and love to lift up the world. Now more than ever.

It is ours to put the mind of God to work. It's what we are here to do. We do it by giving It as many outlets for blessings and healings as we can through our thoughts and actions. This is deliberate work and it is very powerful. Turn your best and highest over to Spirit and then work with what's right in front of you to do. Look for Spirit's handiwork in your life. For every pebble of evidence you see, rejoice—and for heaven's sake don't run around blabbing about it to everyone.

It's up to me, "to see myself as the blessing of Spirit for myself and for the world."

To nurture, honor and protect myself. To know what it is in my life that allows me to thrive, and to make sure that I have that in abundance.

To put myself out there and not hide my light under a bushel but to speak my truth from my heart and soul.

To think of the best part of myself.

To avoid swallowing bugs.

To be the most joyous, loving, supportive Southern Comfort that Spirit is calling me to be.

Take this prayer with you and go watch a sunrise.

Affirmative Prayer

Good harmonizes my mind so that Love sings in my heart. I am completely conscious of the All-Good in me. I am in complete unity with It. I release any idea of lack or limitation. Those ideas are shadows of the truth and like shadows they disappear in the radiance of this right knowing.

My Elbow

Now our Science of Mind teaching has an interesting concept about why we were created.

We were created for the sheer joy of it. It really makes sense if you think about it because why would God do anything it didn't want to do?

God is self-employed so there is no timecard. It only does exactly what It is thrilled to do—nothing more and nothing less.

You and I were an idea in the mind of God before we were anything at all. We were the best idea God had at that moment because God can't have anything but perfect ideas. If God ever had an idea that was less than perfect, it would cease to be

God. It would become one of your relatives that knows everything.

We had a brother-in-law in my family like that. My sister, not the one who married him, would say you could bring up any topic—for example "my elbow"—and likely as not you would have to endure a lengthy dissertation from him on the peculiarities and failures of "your elbow." She didn't actually use elbow as her example but this is a spiritual book so I have to do some cleaning up.

Now, getting back to Spirit, God was so delighted with the idea of you that it thought you into form. All God has to do is contemplate an idea and it shows up in the physical.

Spirit has never been disappointed in you or doubted you for a single moment. It has had far more compassion with your failings and struggles then you've had for yourself.

It is far more interested in your possibilities than any of your mistakes—any of your sins. In fact, Spirit has never paid attention to your sins. How could it? It doesn't know mistakes. It's never made one. Spirit is not concerned with your failings; instead, it is fascinated by your potential.

One of my nieces had such a struggle to have a child. When the little guy finally arrived, I remember just seeing the absolute wonder his two parents had watching him take his first steps.

That's just how much Spirit is in awe of us when we choose to seek love, even though our hearts have been broken countless times. When we choose to try again after failures. When we make the decision to choose happiness over despair, we are setting ourselves in the flow of the creative energies which put the universe in motion.

When we are dwelling in our negativity, we are the only ones generating the energy and it's depleting. It leads to nothing but unhappiness and illness. If you stick with it long enough, eventually the body decides I've had enough of this and I'm out of here.

We were created from joy; we have a spark of divine joy within us. We can focus on it and in doing so the storehouse of heaven will rain down blessings upon us.

Daily life can sometimes wear us down. This short prayer is a good reminder of our purpose for being here, so that God can be God by means of us. It's also a great visual of what we've come to do, to let go of our earthly worries so we can soar into the loving arms of God.

Affirmative Prayer

Every blessing attends my footsteps. I know I am guided onto right paths and that only good can come to me. Spirit directs my journey. I let go of my need to have total control. I turn loose of the trapeze and soar through the air in faith. I let God be God by means of me.

An Italian Cruiser

Here are some tools you can use to open your eyes to the happiness in your life.

First, set your intention to be happy. Many don't. They've given up the goal of being happy because they've been disappointed in the past. Then they go around trying to convince everyone else that they should be unhappy as well. Don't believe it. Have a short affirmation that you can say to yourself all through the day. Life is glorious. God is good. I am happy.

Acknowledge those moments when you are happy. This is very powerful. We often view happiness in the rearview mirror.

I was happy in college, that's good, but it's more powerful to acknowledge I am happy now.

When we acknowledge our happiness in the present moment, we place ourselves in a vortex of creation.

When I'm looking over the new plants in my backyard, I am happy. When I am out with friends, I am happy. Cooking dinner, I am happy. Actually, when I'm microwaving it, but that's another story.

Now if you're in the moment and you're saying, "this is just perfect," if you want some extra points, take a moment and envision something even greater.

Spirit is forever creating and it is attracted to the new, fresh, dynamic and big ideas. Spirit likes a challenge. So, when you're in that moment of high vibration of happiness, use it to co-create with God an even greater life.

Envision what you would be thrilled to have. It's really powerful if you can think of something that you would really love to have, while at the same time knowing you're still happy exactly where you are. That is the sweet spot of cosmic creation to envision something amazing while feeling blessed.

Go for the big, don't worry and let Spirit take it over. You may or may not get the really big thing but you will get something that will match the emotional vibration.

Here's an example: I'm out admiring my back yard, feeling

good and so I envision taking a tour of Europe on an Italian cruise liner.

I've acknowledged my happiness. I throw a vision of even greater joy into Universal Mind. Now, if you really want to add some jet fuel to your cosmic wish wrap it up by thinking of someone who needs a blessing, a healing or a miracle.

I'm in my back yard loving it. I throw a vision of me on an Italian cruise ship and then I wrap it up by seeing my friend who is healing from cancer riding a bike through her neighborhood with a basket full of flowers.

Bless what you have, envision something greater, send love to someone close to you. Three steps: you can do it and it can change your world!

It's called a prayer practice, but that doesn't mean that is has to be painful or joyless. Create a special time for yourself each day when you can contemplate the blessings of life.

Affirmative Prayer

My eyes can see more clearly as I look out upon a broader horizon. Letting go of that which is little, I enter into a larger concept of life. Today I envision my life working well. I laugh often and have fun with my friends and family, dancing whenever and however I can. I live life well and fully.

Angel on Earth

For my birthday one year, my niece gave me tickets to the Dolly Parton concert. What a show that woman puts on! She sang, talked, laughed and played every instrument from the banjo to the Appalachian dulcimer and even with her finger nails. Her great talent, beyond writing, singing and acting, is being able to make an Amphitheater full of strangers feel as though they are visiting with their best friend around a kitchen table.

I'm not sure if Dolly knows the first thing about Science of Mind but she's certainly living it. I was surprised at the number of spiritual songs she sang, even adding a sacred flavor to songs that I had never considered spiritual.

She said of her last CD (Better Day) that she wanted to put together a collection of hopeful songs and she certainly has. The first track on the CD is, *In the Meantime*.

"People have been talking about the end of time ever since time began.

We've been living in the last days, ever since the first day, ever since the dawn of Man

Nobody knows when the end is coming, although some people say they do.

Well it may be today or tomorrow or in a million years or two

In the meantime, in the between time, let us make time to make it right.

And let us not fear what is not clear;

Faith should be your guide.

Think about life, think about living, think about love—caring and giving.

Drop the doomsday attitude and let Spirit flow.

These are wonderful times we're living in.

Eden's garden waits within, so let the flowers grow."

Not only does Dolly sing about making life better, she is also doing her part to make it happen. In 1995, she began the Imagination Library with a commitment to mail a book to every child under five years old in Sevier County, TN (her birth place).

Her program has been so successful that it now sends over a half million books each month to kids enrolled in the program all over the world.

Years ago, Dolly played an angel on the *Designing Women* TV program. There are kids right now who have been born in circumstances where there is not enough time or money to show them the attention they need. For some of these children the only encouragement they get is a book each month from Dolly's organization. With nothing more than a paperback copy of *The Little Engine That Could*, many of these youngsters are going to find a way to overcome every obstacle life throws at them. For those brave little souls, Dolly Parton is a true angel on earth.

"Think about love, think about living, think about love—caring and giving. Drop the doomsday attitude and let Spirit flow." Say this prayer when you want to feel the abundance of God's love flowing in your life.

Affirmative Prayer

God's Love always embraces us. Wisdom is always within us. Joy is ours to share. Abundance is everywhere. I look for it. I see it in others. I do my part to share it with all those around me. I am grateful wherever I see the prosperity of Spirit bringing joy and comfort. In God's mansion there are many rooms.

Sensible Underwear

Dr. Kennedy Shultz, the founder of the Spiritual Living Center of Atlanta, had a very simple answer to the secret of life: "sensible underwear." Certainly, there are some practical applications.

You don't want to be like my sister—not the beauty queen, but the wild child. After one of her divorces she wanted to shake things up some. I was hoping she might try a pottery class or yoga. Instead she announced that she was switching to wearing thongs.

Later, rather foolishly on my part, I asked how the experiment was going. She said she had given them up because a pair had gotten lost. I asked for no further details. Not asking for more bad news is a great practice when dealing with family and friends. They will give you what they want to share, but don't encourage them to give more.

Like when you go to visit someone in the hospital it's very tempting to ask, "What does the doctor say?"

Why ask? It only makes them relive the diagnosis which they're probably already doing too much. Hearing the diagnosis will only cause the idea of them as a sick person to sink more deeply into your consciousness, and theirs.

The best thing, if you really want to help, is to share a fun memory the two of you have where you were playing, laughing or dancing. Then assure them you're going to do something even better when they're well.

When you think of them in the future, it's natural to have the image of them in the hospital bed pop up in your memory. Do all you can to consciously create a vision of them doing something fun. Put yourself in the picture and deliberately remind yourself of it as often as you can. Give gratitude to Spirit for your friend and the fun you're going to have.

What you're doing is actually a prayer—a thing alive with the Spirit of God. Hold onto it with faith. No matter the circumstance, keep true north. Miracles can happen. They do happen all the time regardless of what the experts say. And having a friend to love you, support you, and

think the best of you is nothing short
of a miracle itself.

Like sensible underwear this prayer is essentially about self-love. You can't love God if you don't love yourself. You cannot criticize yourself to enlighten. See yourself as Spirit sees you— wonderous beyond words.

Affirmative Prayer

I walk in the light of God's love. There is an inspiration within me that governs every act and thought. I let go of all worry and doubt. My destination is guaranteed. I have come from love; I live in love and I will return to love. If there is some part of me that I find hard to love, I turn that part over to God. I look for

people to love in my life. I send
love to my world and all in it.
Life responds to my generosity
in full measure, shaken down
and overflowing.

Licking My Hand

What is the secret of life? Well, there is all sort of guidance going around. I know several years ago this movie came out and it offered a rather flippant explanation of how life works. All you have to do is to pray and believe and anything you wanted in life could be yours. You could look at a necklace in the window and *bazzam!* it was around your neck.

Life is a little more complicated. Sometimes through prayers we can produce miraculous results, yet other times, even with our best efforts, we don't get what we desperately desire and sometimes need.

I think of prayer and life like a mighty river.

There is a greater path that we might not understand. We only have the experience of where we are. We don't know where the river is flowing and we don't have a full comprehension of its source.

At some places we have to accept it and go with the flow. Sometimes, it is beyond our control and we have to move to safety.

Where I am right now in my life, the secret for me is sensing where the energy of life wants to flow, then deciding how to use my focus and intention to facilitate my vision. I also have to be willing to work with what shows up. What shows up isn't always what I've imagined. Sometimes it can be far greater than

I've hoped for but it's often different.

One of the people I greatly admire is Betty White. She seems like a lovely person. She likes animals, she's a member of the Unity Church, which is very similar to my teaching, and she has had some of the best pioneer roles of comedy on TV. She keeps reinventing herself, and to me that is one of the biggest challenges of life.

One of my favorite roles she played was Sue Ann Nivens, the tramp on the Mary Tyler Moore show. There's an episode where Mary is throwing a party for Johnny Carson. On the series a running gag was that Mary gave awful parties. None of Mary's friends believed that she actually knew Johnny so they all show up hoping to prove her wrong.

The night of the party there is a huge snow storm in Minneapolis. Everyone is there except Johnny. There's a knock on the door, and everyone assumes it's him. Just as Mary answers the door the lights go out. For the next several minutes all you see is a dark screen while you hear the voices of Mary and Johnny.

At one-point, Johnny ask Mary if he she has a large dog. "No," she replies. "Why do you ask?" "Well," Johnny answers reluctantly, "because I think someone must be licking my hand." After a few seconds of silence, Mary screams out: "Sue Ann, get up off the floor!"

I think I fell in love with the news media perhaps because of Mary Tyler Moore. Unfortunately, like many of us, I am consuming way too much news. This is a good prayer to say after listening to or reading too much of the news.

Affirmative Prayer

There is within me a knowing that is completely conscious of its unity with good. I allow this knowing to flow out into my world. I breathe faith into the greater possibilities of my life. I step out and I step up. I proclaim a world that is turning to love, wisdom and unity. A new day is dawning for humanity. This is the time and now is the generation.

A Secret of Life

Later on, Betty had a wonderful role on the *Golden Girls* and then, I feel, had an overlooked run on *Hot in Cleveland*.

The *Golden Girls* while being a funny show, from what I understand, was a really miserable place to work. I find it interesting that some shows that have brought great joy weren't fun to produce. *I Love Lucy*, is another example.

Golden Girls wasn't a happy place for several reasons. Estelle Getty, who played the mom, was suffering the beginning effects of Alzheimer's. She had trouble remembering her lines and was very stressed.

While people almost universally liked Betty, Bea Arthur, who played Dorothy and was the star of the show, totally hated her. I think she may have disliked Betty's sunny disposition and that she didn't take herself so seriously. Bea thought acting had to be work and if you were having fun at it you weren't taking it seriously enough.

Betty knew Bea didn't like her and she didn't understand it. She made an effort to be friendly but she didn't let it become the focal point of her life. Regardless of Bea, she went on to have a wonderful time. She let Bea have her own problems and didn't take them on for herself.

Now, there's a secret of life for you. She could have allowed Bea's behavior to ruin her good time, to change her opinion of herself, or even change her behavior. Instead, she stayed a nice person, having a glorious life. Now that Bea Arthur has gone on, everyone totally agrees that Betty White is universally loved.

This short prayer will help you feel the oneness with your soul and the All Good. In this place we accept the truth about ourselves and can easily release anyone's negative opinion of us.
Terry Cole-Whittaker wrote a book titled, "What You Think of Me is
None of My Business."
Use this prayer to release negative opinions.

Affirmative Prayer

I know that the Spirit of Truth is within me.
I contact this Spirit through my own
self-recognition. Good harmonizes my mind, so that Love sings joyously in my

heart. I am completely conscious of All Good in me and around me. I lift up my cup of acceptance knowing that the Divine outpouring will fill it to the brim.

The Time is Now

Claiming our good requires an active role on our part. The entire point of our experience is to see ourselves as vital in the creation of our good. To become one with the creative energy which created us, we should see ourselves blessed in more good of every kind.

Make it a point to see everyone in your life doing better, even those that bother you to no end—particularly those who bother you. By thinking well of them, they'll either start having a more blessed life and improve their behavior or you'll start having so much fun in your life that you will pay them less attention.

The time is now; the place is where we are. Many of us can go through much of our lives putting our goals off for another day. We avoid the step by step process that would be required if our goals were to come to us in a natural way. Imagine that you want to be a movie star. You can wait until the magic fairy sneaks through your window one night to give you the looks of a young Robert Redford with the talent of Robert De Niro. Or you can take acting classes.

When we put off our dreams, we allow ourselves the hallucination of what could be and, in that place, we can spend a lifetime. When we start moving on our dreams our pathway opens up.

If you want to be an actor, then get involved in community theater.

Perhaps in your first performance of *Fiddler on the Roof* a powerful Hollywood agent will be in attendance. Or, perhaps the actor playing your co-star is the love of your life and the two of you create a loving and passionate relationship that the red carpet and bright lights of a movie opening could never match.

Either way you will learn that you and your desires are a vital part of creation and once you have learned that lesson for yourself there is nothing that can stand in your way.

Like the fiddler on the roof you have come to play your song of life for all who will hear. High above the turmoil and confusion of everyday life, the roof is not as scary as it looks. Say this prayer and step up and out to a larger you. The world is waiting to hear your song.

Affirmative Prayer

God's Love always embraces us. God's Wisdom is always within us. Its Joy is ours to share. Abundance is everywhere. So, as I move out into my world, I will look for that which supports this truth. I will turn away from any idea that goodness and prosperity are not my birthright. I will not sell myself short. I deserve the great good of my health, of an overflowing bank account. I deserve a purpose and passion in my life. I am here to be something, to say something or to know something. I am here to make a joyful noise to the Lord with my laughter, joy and love.

A Fruity Chardonnay

In my childhood, Sundays were a day of dread because we were all forcibly hauled off to Napier Avenue Church of God. Now strangely enough my parents never joined the Church or professed having a born-again experience. The born-again experience was a requirement for getting into heaven and bypassing hell. So, each week we went to Church where we were all told in no uncertain terms that we were headed to an everlasting diet of brimstone.

Our misery started out each Sunday with my father turning up the volume on the TV as loud as possible for a gospel program called the *Happy Goodman Family*. If I or one of my sisters could have gotten our hands around their pudgy little necks, none of them would have been happy for long.

The star of the program was Vesta Goodman. She was what we called in the South, big boned. She had a hairdo like the soft served ice cream from Dairy Queen. It just kept building on itself in layers. Fortunately, she chose to forgo the little curl on top. Vesta's fame came because she could really belt out a song. And she seemed happy doing it. She really enjoyed singing.

The theme song of the show was *Jubilee*—"Join us in this happy jubilee." I always envisioned a merry caravan off to see the world and to have fun. In many ways that kind of describes Jesus and his disciplines.

What I never was taught at the Napier Avenue Church of God was that it was through a celebration that Jesus stepped into his power. He was at a wedding when they ran out of wine and his mom came and told him to make more. He wanted to fuss, but being the good Jewish mother that she was she would have none of it. She instructed the servants to start setting up the jars of water. In scripture it is plural—not one jar mind you.

Could you imagine having to make wine for your Jewish mom? I can just see her giving him instructions. "I want a fruity chardonnay here, a dry sauvignon there." I am sure that after satisfying his mom, aunts and their friends with wine, that healing the lame and raising the dead had to be a piece of cake for Jesus.

Here's the point: Jesus had to be encouraged to step into his power. We all need encouragement to step into the greater part of ourselves and we need someone reminding us that we can do it.

This is why it's so important to find a spiritual community where you are encouraged to live with more joy, enthusiasm and inspiration and a place where you feel better for having gone. Where you are reminded that within you is a Spirit filled possibility which can bring more life, more joy and more happiness into the world.

**It was Marianne Williamson who said,
"Our deepest fear is not that we are inadequate. Our deepest fear is that we are powerful beyond measure."
This is a prayer for when, just like Jesus,
you need a little nudge to step up to the better part of yourself.**

Affirmative Prayer

Today, I rest in divine assurance and divine security. I know that all is well with my soul, my spirit and my mind. All is well with my affairs. I let go of every thought of worry. I take care of what needs to be taken care of and then I turn my affairs over to Spirit. I am not in the world on my own. I have a friend and partner who believes in me, who tirelessly works for my good. I do my best. I rest completely in the truth that Spirit loves, supports and encourages every idea for my living the best life possible.

A Joyful Noise

True spirituality is to help us make a joyful noise. Jesus came to life so that we might have more life. So, when we are bringing more joy to life, we are in the energetic flow of Christ consciousness. This is the vortex of creation, the power of life, to encourage, to inspire and to uplift, starting with ourselves.

Want a greater life? Get a better idea about God. Get a better idea about yourself and that better idea is what you deserve. It is Spirit approved and Spirit ordained.

We don't get in life what we need or wish, but we do get what we think we deserve.

So, think of yourself: "I deserve an overflowing bank account. I deserve a flexible comfortable body with energy so I can do the things I need to do, and then do the things that are fun. I deserve to have family and friends who encourage me to play, to laugh so hard that I have to catch my breath. I deserve to have meaning in my life and to know that I am a part of something greater than myself. To know the world is a better place because I am in it."

If you will put these ideas about yourself into the Universal Mind, you will find yourself in a partnership with life, with God— with good. Then celebrate it however you see it showing up, and expand your ways of seeing it. Cast your net far and wide.

This is a great prayer to know something better for yourself: God can't until you do. I love, love the idea, "Nothing is impossible for God and nothing is impossible for me." Say it to yourself as often as you can and you will amaze yourself with the bounty of Life.

Affirmative Prayer

I let go of thoughts of fear and doubt. The future is bright with hope and fulfillment. The present is perfect and no past failure mars today's joy. I know that my life is the Perfect Life of Spirit. I now permit It to radiate through my world of thought and action. Nothing is

impossible for God and
nothing is impossible for me. I
release all false ideas that have
held me in bondage.
I unite myself with faith and
joy.
I live without fear.

Fizzy Well Water

Sometimes, miracles come as a blessing and sometimes they come by way of us saving ourselves a boat load of trouble.

Harry Truman used to say that for every three troubles you see coming down the road toward you, two will run in the ditch before they get to you. He also said, "Never kick a fresh cow patty on a hot summer's day." He was a man of uncommon wisdom.

Last week I was in a rush. On my way to the office, I went to the refrigerator to grab one of my kombucha teas. I brew my own. It's quite the experiment. If you're not familiar with kombucha, it's fermented tea made with yeast. My partner calls it a fungus.

I keep it in the refrigerator in our garage, because my partner is not going to allow a fungus to grow in our house. So, we keep it outside with no questions asked.

The refrigerator we store it in has moveable drawers in the door. I had one bottle of tea left and it was in the side drawer which was packed with long neck glass bottles of what our neighbor lady likes to drink. We love our little neighbor lady so we keep her drink of choice in the house, cold and ready to go.

Her drink is a variety of hard lemonades that have become popular in the last couple of years. That in itself is not too bad, but she likes the diet ones, which is like drinking fizzy well water. If you don't know what well water tastes like, just imagine drinking water from a lead pipe. They have flavors like berry and cherry which taste like cough medicine made with well water… fizzy.

In my haste to be on my way, I grabbed the last of my teas when the entire drawer lifted up. For a moment, I was holding in midair a drawer packed with long neck bottles of artificially sweet, cherry flavored, fizzy diet lemonade. Time slowed down as I envisioned the broken glass mess I was about to have on our garage floor. And in a flash, without me giving it a single thought, I shoved all the contents onto the main shelf of the fridge, diverting a tragedy.

"Thank you, Jesus!" I yelled out while giving gratitude for the wisdom which had come to me to solve the problem. It had come in a flash from somewhere other than my conscious mind. I hadn't even realized that the shelf was empty.

There is a wisdom of the universe that we can access. There is an intelligence that we can use to make our lives flow better without so much muss and fuss, stress and strain and turmoil.

It comes more easily to us when we are in a neutral place in life, when we are not striving so hard to make something happen, and when we are not mournfully looking back on what could have been. When we're in a neutral place where we're content where we are and expecting better to come along.

This is a great prayer if we want to feel better about the people in our lives. The more we see the goodness of Spirit in the lives of those around us, the more we will have it in our own lives.

Affirmative Prayer

In all I do I seek to be of service and assistance to others. The kingdom of God is at hand today and I enter into it with joy. I will look for the good in those around me. I will quickly and adamantly dismiss any negative intent. I will know better for them even when they can't know it for themselves. I will see the Glory of God's love and creativity reflected in the eyes of all. I will look out on the creation of my life and I will proclaim, "This is Good".

Kvetching

There is something of Spirit that wants to be born in your life. Look and listen, there is something in your life calling to you.

I go out walking in the morning while the cicadas are still singing, and I think to myself, what are they singing to me? What is it in my soul that wants to join their choirs?

What is it in me that wants to sing out in joy? If it's not in joy, it's not of Spirit.

If it brings good to me, harms no one, it must be of Spirit and it is my Father's and Mother's good blessing to bring it to life by means of me.

I, of myself, can do nothing, but in Spirit I can move mountains.

We all have this power when we choose to lift our eyes to a better knowing.

To join the chorus of life and to declare our lives a jubilee. Free of cosmic debt and not taking on any more. We are on the move. We do it through our joy, our laughter, our support of one another and our lifting of one another. Holding the high watch for ourselves and each other by making life a celebration of the good, the wholesome and the Godly in all of us.

So, get out there and you be you. Do what you have come to life to do. Stop your whining and your kvetching. Step into your power.

Bring a joyful noise unto the Lord. Because the party has just begun, you're up for a miracle, and Momma needs a fruity chardonnay.

Use this prayer when you want to feel more love in your life. The nice thing about love is that you can always give more of it. Be sure to smile at your cashier, thank a postman or better yet, donate some money to your local pet rescue and go pet a kitten or let a puppy lick your nose.

Affirmative Prayer

Peace and joy exist and they are mine. I love and am loved. In joy, then, I greet each day and rest at night with a calm confidence in Spirit. Today my faith, hope and expectancy look up and out. I behold a limitless love giving of itself to everything and an infinite peace enveloping all. I accept the wholeness of Spirit. I identify myself and everything that I am with the harmony and perfection of the Life of God.

A Visitor from Charleston

The week before I left Atlanta for St. Augustine, I was walking the dogs late one night when I saw a lone figure coming up the hill in front of our house. It was a humid night and the street light cast an eerie glow. I could tell this person had a dog, so I crossed to the other side of the street. I never knew how Buddy (a doggie guest in our house) and Sadie would respond to a stranger. Huge Buddy was likely to jump up on their shoulders while trying to lick their faces and Sadie was just as likely to attack their toes with the tenacity of fresh water piranhas.

My plan backfired when the approaching dog ran out to meet us. "Are they friendly," his walker called out. "Sure," I answered hopefully. Actually, they were so calm and friendly that I wondered if I had the right dogs.

Sarah, as she introduced herself, was visiting from Asheville. She had grown up in the neighborhood. Asking where I lived, she remembered the Orensteins who use to own our house. Then without much warning, she blurted out, "My father died last night." She almost surprised herself by saying it and you could tell she wasn't yet comfortable with it.

She told me that he had been in his nineties and that the only thing keeping him going was his feeling that he had to make sure his wife would be cared for. He was able to stay at home until the last 24 hours. When they took him into hospice on

Tuesday, she had rushed down from Asheville to be with him.

Her mother was too frail to leave the house and her brother was sick with the flu, so she was the only one who could visit. Once at his bedside she wanted him to know she would take care of her Mom. She said that the only thing she knew to do was to crawl into bed with him and start singing the Bob Marley song, "*Everything's Gonna be Alright*."

She said when she finished her song, he pushed her hand away and took one last breath. The nurse in the room said that when he released her hand it was his way of acknowledging that he was ready to move on. We talked for another moment or so, and I asked her to visit us before she left.

As we walked away, I blurted out something that I was surprised to hear myself say. "He's so proud of you, you know." I don't know why I said it, but I felt like I would burst if I didn't. There were tears in her eyes and tears in mine. I was something of an emotional wreck and it took the two dogs to lead me back home. For a long time, I sat by the front door watching the night sky thinking of my encounter.

It was one of those conversations that occur completely at happenstance. You never know when they will happen or who they will be with, but you know it is a moment that will stay with you for the rest of your life. When I think of Sarah, I hope I will remember her courage, love and conviction that Everything Will Be Alright. An idea that got her through an all too worldly moment with enough compassion to open wide the gates of heaven.

The biggest assurance we can give to ourselves and each other is "Everything's gonna be alright." It really is what we need to know and essentially the request and the answer to every prayer. If you're feeling a bit unsure about your future, use this prayer.

Affirmative Prayer

I focus my vision on the indwelling harmony, knowing that as I contemplate this inward perfection, I shall manifest peace in my life. There is nothing in the external world which can rob me of my equilibrium. Spirit created me with the calmness of a right idea. I harmonize my life to that idea—that Love is powerful; kindness can overcome hatred and compassion is the unmovable force of the Universe. Why should I fret or worry? God's eye is on the sparrow and I know It watches me.

Roy Rogers Cowboy Boots

If the seed saw dirt as the enemy, the oak would never grow because the soil has the very nutrients needed to allow the tree to reach its great height. Often the thing which we feel is holding us back is the very thing we need to provide us with the courage and the strength to move forward. Barriers either will keep us imprisoned or give us the strength and vision to grow to the heavens. In our thinking, barriers can become the invisible prisons of our minds. They are "no thing" trying to become something at our expense.

When I look back on my life, what I thought were barriers were "no thing". They were things that I had come up with in my mind to keep me living a limited experience. For twenty years, I stayed in a soul numbing job because I was convinced that I wouldn't know what to do without it. When I finally quit, being indecisive about my next move was not a problem. It was never really a problem anyway except in my own thinking. There were real barriers that confronted me but many of them I didn't acknowledge. I managed to move past them without a moment's notice.

In my childhood hometown of Macon, Georgia, there was a good bit of class prejudice. My family was definitely on the wrong side of the track and we didn't really make much of an effort to prove otherwise. Our neighborhood was on the edge of a good neighborhood morphing into a bad one. I paid no mind to any of it, because I knew something was better out there. I was convinced that the real world was what I saw on TV, where moms arranged fresh cut flowers, and during the holidays families gathered around the piano to sing Christmas carols. My family had none of this but as long as I75 North remained open, I told myself, I would make it out.

Looking back, I almost have to thank someone who wasn't so nice to me for actually giving me this gift—Mrs. Patterson. If our house was just on the edge of the wrong side of the neighborhood, Mrs. Patterson's was just on the edge of the right side. And she was desperate to get as far removed from our side as possible.

Mrs. Patterson and her husband had adopted a son. It was supposed to be a secret but everyone knew it. She had perfectly white hair and she told people that it turned white overnight when her son, Mark, had experienced a life-threatening illness. Everyone knew it was a lie, but we went along with it anyway.

Mark survived his illness, but he lived a regimented life under his mom's total control. Their house was really nice, much more like the ones I saw on television. His room was filled with all sorts of great games but his mom wouldn't let you play with them unless she watched. Even then she made you play by the rules.

Sometimes, she would give us cookies and lemonade as a snack.

She would use me as an example for Mark on how not to eat cookies or drink lemonade. My sister Sandra said it was just like some white-headed bitch to give somebody something really good to eat and then not let them enjoy it.

Anyway, I didn't allow this to bother me. Even though Mark could be sort of a jerk. I always felt sorry for him not having a real mom of his own. I was always hopeful that his real parents would come back to rescue him. On top of that, I had the kryptonite to ruin Mrs. Patterson's life and as a five-year-old kid I knew it.

My power lay in my pair of Roy Rogers cowboy boots which had the ability to leave an awful scuff mark on Mrs. P's prized possession of her polished linoleum kitchen floor. I could send her into apoplectic fits as I would do the cha-cha across her floor. No dancer on *Dancing with the Stars* could ever go as fast and as hard as I could with sheer mayhem and delight.

This is a prayer for taking back and knowing your strength, when you've really had a tough day. Before you curl up in your most comfortable PJs and turn on the TV, say this prayer for yourself. Tomorrow will be better and even if the situation doesn't improve you will. A better you will always provide a better way.

Affirmative Prayer

I know that the Spirit of God has made me, and the breath of the Almighty has given me life. I feel at home with God. I know I am a conduit for the love of God, the goodness of Spirit and the prosperity of Universal Creativity. I am a perfect idea in the mind of God and I have come to life to manifest that idea. I know there is absolutely never a problem in life that God and I can't solve. God and I equal a majority in every situation. I can look out on a world of problems and say, "You're not the boss of me." I have a power and knowing within my soul. I have not come from star dust to be a victim. I am here to know the greatest love and joy that Spirit has in my hopes and dreams.

Shout Glory

So, we have barriers—some real, some perceived. We can give power to them, but there is something in us that will allow us to overcome them in one way or another. It might not be the way we choose, but Spirit will provide us a path.

I heard a story this week about two friends, one a runner and the other a wounded military veteran in a wheelchair. The runner pushed his friend across country. I wouldn't even want to drive across country, but here this guy did it pushing a wheelchair.

And I thought of the consciousness of his friend. I'm sure he would have preferred to run himself, but then I thought of the love he must have felt knowing he had someone who cared for him that much.

They thought it was just a cross country run but Spirit had greater plans. Now their story has gone viral—read by millions and inspiring even more.

Spirit has great plans for us. To be our best self and to make a difference where we are.

When we leave to go on to a bigger and better experience, if we have done what we could with what we have here, we'll get more opportunities in the life that follows.

You plus God equals an answer to every problem you have. Your desires come from your source so there is a way for them to be made manifest. Your real desires are channels of the energy that created the universe. So, there is a way for them to breathe the air of life. We are bigger, greater and more powerful than we have ever imaged ourselves to be.

The biggest barrier we have is ourselves in our limited thinking.

My teacher said he would look in the mirror and say, "You're the biggest problem I have."

It's a good thing, because if we are our biggest problem, we can change it. We can change our thinking. To me the easiest way is through Affirmative Prayer.

Decide what it is you want in your life. Be able to describe it in such terms that you can get a visual of it in your mind with you in it. Spend enough time thinking about it until you feel a wave of energy. Release it to Spirit and say this is done, because I have turned it over to God.

Act about it the same way you would when you put something in the microwave. You don't stand there staring at it like we used to when microwaves first came out. Now you turn it on and you go about your business.

Do that with your prayer. Put it into the mind of God and go on about your business.

Then look out on the world and when you feel it for a moment and you see any sign of it, shout, "Glory". Then you look for others either having what you desire or achieving what you want and give thanks for it. If the good you are seeking comes to anyone, it can come to you.

We are living in an intelligent universe which responds to our mental state. To the extent that we learn to control our thinking, we control our lives. We must let this great power operate though us. What we outwardly are, and what we are to become depends upon what we are thinking. What you are thinking now is important.

Deliberate thought is the most powerful of all. When you deliberately say, "Yes I could spend the next twenty minutes wondering why I have a jerk of a boss, why all politicians are knuckle heads, or whatever, but instead I am going to deliberately think about what good can I bring to my life and to the lives of those around me," you have placed yourself in a current of great energy. You can do it. It doesn't have to be a huge sacrifice. It can be just as simple as being pleasant and encouraging.

The barrier to our good is that we see ourselves and the world as form. We don't realize the great power we have by being spiritual beings. Thought attracts what is like itself and repels what is unlike itself. Let us then enlarge our thought process and dare to think in universal terms for our good and for all those we see and have interactions with.

Say this prayer when you are seeking a God inspired idea in your life. The best way Spirit has to communicate with us is through our greater ideas about ourselves. God knows better for you so isn't it time to know better for yourself? This is a great prayer for first thing in the morning.

Affirmative Prayer

I know that Life gives to me according to my faith. Today I elevate my faith and mind. I engage Spirit as It flows through me with inspiration. I say, "Yes" to every idea that God provides. I keep them in sacred trust with Spirit. I look for the subtle indications that

I'm on the right track. When I see even the smallest signs of God's support I shout, "Glory!" I give thanks for those around me who are achieving the good I seek. I know that if Spirit has ever answered any prayer, it must answer mine. I am grateful for this right knowing and I release this prayer into the mind of God.

Plenty O' Dogs

I got a call this week from one of my relatives. It was one of those calls that when you see the name on the phone you want to light a candle and sprinkle salt around your chair just to make it spooky.

So, this relative has wanted a new man in her life for seven years. She has gone from one loser to the next. When she begins telling me about the newest guy, I can't help but think: "Oh, Lord not another one— we're on double digits now."

Early on I tried talking her into going on E-Harmony, but she doesn't want to have to pay to meet the man she's hoping to spend the rest of her life with. So instead she's on a free website called Plenty O'

291

Dogs. It fairly reeks of romance, doesn't it?

The last of her hopefuls she introduced me to was nice enough. He wanted me to call him by his nickname which was "Nine Toes." He had an accident at work which helped him get on disability. It had left him without a pinky toe but on the government dole. He thought it was a fair bargain. He tried taking off his shoe to prove it, but I begged off.

Fortunately, Mr. Nine Toes didn't last very long. So, I'm listening to her about the latest catch and I start thinking, "Here we go again." But I catch myself. "Wait a minute," I thought, "she deserves love." There are plenty o' dogs out there, someone nice, with most of their body parts. This could be it, so let me put my energy into that idea. It will do her, me and even Mr. Nine Toes, wherever he may be, a great deal of good.

There is no limitation to our good, except that which we accept. We all can think of something better than we have so far experienced in our lives. We have the ability to go beyond our best experiences and rise triumphant above them.

Since you have the idea of your good, it follows that there is already a mechanism in the universe to bring that good to you.

To connect to the wholeness of ourselves, and the fulness of ourselves.

To unite with our good and see the barriers as that thing which is allowing us to soar.

So, if you have a barrier of someone or something telling you that you are not worthy or deserving, just know that you have a pair of your very own Roy Rogers cowboy boots within your soul. That decision alone can give you the strength, power and courage to cha-cha yourself across any problem or barrier you perceive right to the very gates of heaven.

This is the truth in your life and it is the truth in mine, and so it is.

One last word: Remember, your life is not a problem to be solved, it is a miracle unfolding. It is your job to go name your miracle, proclaim your miracle, and to make it your own.

God Bless Us All.

Biography

Ken is senior minister of the Center for Spiritual Living in St. Augustine, Florida. He lives with his partner of over twenty-years and their two dogs. They live in an amazing community where people are actually friendly with one another.

Ken leads an active community in St. Augustine. Each year they help buy school supplies for kids in need. They provide Christmas to people in nursing homes and children. They are active in the Interfaith movement. They provide scholarships to kids with special challenges, and have just begun a service to help battered women see themselves in a different light.

Services are full, funny, inspiring and packed with great music. You'll also find a lovely group of people. You will leave feeling better about yourself.

If you're planning a trip to St. Augustine, please plan to join us on Sundays at 10:00 AM. You can watch one of Rev. Ken's services by going to: cslstaugustine.org.

Cover artwork by:
Marleen Block
Contact artsymarlena@gmail.com

Made in the USA
Columbia, SC
23 November 2019